CITISCAPE

BY

BEV SCHLOENDORF

Copyrights

PROOF OF COPYRIGHT OWNERSHIP

REF NUMBER: 28395030525S051

This certificate should be verified at www.protectmywork.com and not relied upon solely
as PDF or screenshot. Ask the author for a shareable link.

REGISTERED ON	3rd May 2025 At 18:22:02 CET
REGISTERED BY	Beverly Schloendorf
REGISTRATION TYPE	Email
SENDER MAIL CLIENT INFORMATION	Mail-Qt1-F181.Google.Com ([209.85.160.181]:46376)
WORK TITLE	Novel For Copyright

Registration certificate issued & certified by:

Protectmywork Limited
Kemp House, 152 City Road, London, EC1V 2NX, United Kingdom.
Company Registered in England & Wales No. 04358873

CERTIFIED EMAIL DATA

Book Publishers

a

Hampton Publishers

Acknowledgement

To all my friends and family who suffered through this with me--you know who you are

---Thank you.

To my team at Hampton Publishers, thank you for getting this project off the ground for me. Let's hope it's a good journey.

Contents

Preface

Know what makes you happy.

Know what makes you sad.

Know what makes you angry.

Know what makes you glad.

Know the light that lives in you.

Know the secret, dark parts too.

Know the Earth, feel the sky.

Laugh and dance; sing and cry.

Light the fire in your soul

That leads you where you want to go.

Belong. Become. Be part of life.

Live and love in spite of strife.

Be the best YOU you can be.

A heartfelt wish from me

To thee.

Tale 1: A Night in the Life....

Sometimes, I hate my job! Yeah, I know all the reasons why it's necessary: think of all the pain and suffering that would go on endlessly if I didn't do my thing, yada, yada, yada. But there are times when I could throw in the towel and just *QUIT*! Like tonight, for instance.

I stomped down the hospital corridors, my clothes flapping in the moving antiseptic-laced air. Behind me, machines wailed and anguished parents cried, and there was nothing I could do about that. Nurses and doctors in their flashy uniforms raced around, doing what they do best. But there was nothing they could do about it either, except unplug the machines and console the broken-hearted.

It seemed, at that moment, that I was the only being in the universe that got all the blame and never got one shred of comfort. And after doing the friggin' baby run—again-- I could have used it. *I hate the baby run.* Why the *Powers That Be* (PTB) kept giving it to me was a mystery. But as I never actually saw any of the members of that *august* committee, I was never given the opportunity to ask.

Behind me, I could hear the anguished wail of a new father as he begged his God for an answer; the hiccupping sobs of the new mother, mindless with grief. I could hear the thoughts of the medical professionals as they worked over the small, still body, railing at the unfairness of death, and how they hated losing the war against it.

Why do I get the blame? Do they actually suppose that I like coming into their structures of glass and stone and metal and medicine to undo what they have tried so hard to achieve? Why does everyone assume that I have no feelings about what I do? Especially this particular list.

I wonder what they would say if they knew that I tried to make it as painless and quick as possible? That I used every mesmerizing trick I had at my disposal to stop the fear? That I cried too, as I did what was demanded of me?

What would people say if they saw Death standing over a tiny hospital bassinet, weeping? *Bah*!!!! Curse the Powers That Be and their never-ending lists!

I walked out of the building, not bothering tonight to use the doors as I usually did. My frustration and anger were making me edgy and restless, so instead of heading "home", I went for a walk in the park across the street.

Streetlights and fountain lights created little halos of gold along the walkways. But I strode through the darker, unlit areas, letting the blackness surround me. Sometimes this helped. Apparently not tonight, though. I was just another dark shade with no hope of succour or release from his own personal hell.

"Why?" I thought to myself. "What was the point? Why that baby? Why the baby runs at all?" and most of all, "Why me?" Not sure what else to do right then, I plunked myself down on a park bench and stared morosely at the toes of my boots.

My sulk was interrupted by voices.

"They lost another one tonight," a woman's voice said calmly.

"Oh. Poor wee thing," another woman's voice answered, soft and sad. "What happened?"

"No one knows for sure," followed by the crinkle of plastic as she unwrapped something. "Just one of those things, I guess."

"I'll be sure to light a candle for it tomorrow," the second woman opened a plastic something of her own.And then they were quiet as they ate their lunch, and my funk sat deeper in my chest. After a moment, I sighed heavily and dragged myself off the bench and headed for "home".

No. I do not personally work 24/7. There is no way that one entity, no matter how gifted, could be everywhere at once, the world over, doing this work for the PTB. So instead, there are teams of us working in shifts within a given area with a list of people that require our services. Lists that we were not allowed to deviate from for any reason. No matter how repugnant we thought it was. And when we are done, we are allowed to find a place in which to rest until our next shift commences. *Ad infinitum.*

I was still too upset to even think about relaxing, so I spent a little more time and energy wandering the streets and back alleys of the city that was part of my territory. It was late enough in the night (or early enough in the morning) to be called quiet by city standards. A few early delivery vans are making their first run of the day, a store here and there, prepping for the coffee crowd. An all-night store open but not busy, if the clerk was reading on the counter, was any indication. A taxi or two, idling at the curb. A drunk or a derelict sleeping wherever he fell, or was dropped, or pushed.

Not that it's really necessary, because generally I can walk through anything solid, I either step around or over these poor bundles of humanity when I pass them by. *I dunno*. Just seems like the right thing to do. Sometimes they wake up and look around, and shiver as I pass. Most don't. Which is fine with me. I meandered on.

In the vaults of my mind, I kept seeing the tiny face, the rosebud lips, the long golden lashes, the eyelids so thin they were blue from all the little veins, the waxy pale skin. I felt like a murderer. I hated myself. I hated the world. I hated the people in it.

Why? Why? Why?

I came out of my funk and realized that I was no longer in my own familiar territory. In fact, I had no idea where I was. Didn't recognize a single building around me. Stymied, I sat down on the cement steps of a large stone edifice, forgetting for a moment that I could "think" myself back home if I really wanted to. Dawn was just breaking as I sat there. The rosy glow stained the velvet of night and slowly began to bleach it away. Long strips of pink and gold lit the ground between the buildings and the trees and crawled slowly up the steps on which I sat.

Behind me, a heavy wooden door slid open, the wood grinding slightly on the cement and flagstone portico. I thought about looking up, seeing who it was, but decided against it. Why bother? Whoever it was couldn't see me anyway. The person sat down on the top step. I could see polished black shoes and black pants in the corner of my eye. To see the rest of him, I would have to turn and look up. *Meh.*

The guy sucked in a big breath and then let it out in a long sigh. "It isn't easy, is it?" His voice was deep and echoed faintly in the stillness. I didn't answer. He couldn't see me. So, he had no idea I was there and therefore could not be talking to me.

"All the platitudes in the world don't make it any easier either," he continued. "Even knowing that you have to do it, bound by rules and regulations that you can't escape. For reasons that you don't understand. Or are not given," he laid his hand on my shoulder. "Taking it on faith that they know what they are doing."

Wait a minute! He was touching me! No one touches me! Or see me! Or talks to me (except to *blame me*)! I jumped up so fast my shadow stayed behind on the step and had to catch up.

He sat quietly, smiling. His hands, gnarled and wrinkled with arthritis and age, rested in his lap. His black cassock was simple and unadorned. No ribbons, pins, or belts to mark his station. His hair, thinning and very white, floated in a breeze that I wasn't aware of. His face, like his hands, were wrinkled and marked by time and his many joys and sorrows. But the most arresting feature of the man as a whole was his eyes. I supposed that at one time they might have been some colour of blue. Now, however, they were milk white and blinded by cataracts.

"Wondering how I knew you were there?" he asked, waving a hand at his face. "I suppose the simplest answer would be that I could *feel* your confusion and anger. It was coming off of you in waves. So, I joined you out here on the step."

"But...." I spluttered.

"Yes. A mystery. One, I fear neither of us will be able to answer adequately, or honestly." he tilted his head a little and fixed his rheumy eyes on mine. Then waited. Obviously, the next move was up to me. I could teleport to my safety or I could stay and chat a while. I took a step away and then surprised myself and sat down on the step again.

"Okay. Now what?" I asked petulantly.

He laughed. "Has it been so long since you've had a conversation with someone?"

"Well, yeah." belligerently this time.

"Alright. Normally, there would be introductions, but I suppose that doesn't matter much in this instance. So, I suppose the easiest thing would be to ask why you are so troubled and angry," the old guy replied, calm as you please, like having a real chat with Death is an everyday occurrence for him.

And there it was again: all the anger, confusion, hatred, and indignation I felt about my job. Like a volcano, it spewed out of my mouth in a never-ending torrent. And while I spat out all the vitriol, he sat there and calmly listened to it all without interrupting. When I finally ran out of things to yell about, I felt deflated. Empty even.

"Is there nothing about your work that you, well, not enjoy, exactly, but agree with?" he asked quietly.

"Well, yeah. Sure. When someone has been ill for a long time, or lived a full life. Then I don't mind so much." I replied.

"Hmm. So, your real issue then is the baby run, as you call it?"

"Yeah! I mean, seriously! They haven't even been around long enough to learn how to laugh or smile yet. And it seems like I get that job more than most! Sometimes when I close my eyes, I can see them all! Hundreds of little bodies. It makes me wanna puke!"

"And what about the ones who have been around that long and live in pain and fear until you are sent for them?"

"Those ones aren't so bad, honestly. 'Cause I know it's a good thing, really, because they shouldn't have to go through all that. Nobody should."

"True. But that isn't the world we live in, is it? No matter how hard we try, we can't seem to end all the pain and suffering and fear in the world."

"It sucks."

"And when you come for the ones who are the cause of all that pain and suffering?"

"Those ones are easy. I almost enjoy those." I said fiercely, suddenly remembering one particular instance.

Before I knew it, I was telling him the story:

It was another night, not so many years ago, I guess, I was heading towards my next appointment. I was a little early because I didn't recognize the address on my list as a building that I had ever been to before. When I thought I was close, I stopped to look around.

I heard some noises in the alley behind me, and when I turned to see, a little girl came running out onto the sidewalk. She was just a little slip of a thing. Covered in filth and blood. Face as white as a ghost. Eyes as big as saucers and full of tears. She was trying to scream but couldn't make any noise. Maybe because she was so terrified, maybe she couldn't talk. *I dunno*. But she didn't look to be any older than five.

Right behind her, a great lumbering giant of a man came out. Just as filthy and splattered with blood. He reached for the girl and grabbed her hair; made like he was going to drag her back into the alley. She tried fighting him, but he was so big and she was so tiny, it was a no contest.

I remember feeling utterly helpless myself and looking for anything I could do to stop whatever was going to happen. I even tried to get the attention of a passerby up the walk. But either he didn't want to get involved, or he was just plain dumb. He just ran into the first open store and disappeared.

Fortunately, a passing cop car saw the whole thing. I don't think their car was even stopped when they barrelled out the doors, guns out, and ran towards the guy. They ordered him to stop. He kept dragging the kid. They warned him that if he didn't stop, they'd shoot him. He ignored them and started into the alley.

The cops fired. They hit the guy point-blank. But they also hit the girl because, as they went around the corner, he picked her up and slung her over his shoulder like a sack of potatoes. I took her right away. As quickly and carefully as I could. She actually smiled a little as she went.

Him? Him I let feel the burn of the bullet as it ripped through him. I let him feel every drop of blood run out of the gaping wounds. I listened to him scream for mercy and ignored every word. It was slow and it was painful. You can pack a lot of pain into a couple of minutes, Then I took him before the ambulance guys had a chance to get there.

I finished telling the story, saying, "I know I'm not supposed to do it that way. But I'm not sorry I did either."

"So, there is sometimes solace and comfort in what you are given to do. Sometimes, pain and suffering. And sometimes justice as well." calm, nonjudgmental.

"Yeah. I guess."

"So, think again about that poor child."

"What about her?"

"What if, perhaps, you or another had taken her in her sleep as a wee infant? You would have saved her that final torment. Or maybe an even worse fate."

I thought about it.

"Isn't it possible? Neither you nor I knows what the future holds. What Fate, or God, or whomever they believe in has decreed for each person's lifetime." he waited a minute to let that thought sink in. "Maybe it is a mercy you have no understanding or knowledge of when you take them. Rather than letting them suffer needlessly, they are released before they can know anything of the pain and anger, and humiliation of the world. They get to move forward without mental or physical scars to their next life. And one last thing. Do you suppose that *maybe* you seem to get the baby list precisely because you are so gentle and take such care when you do what you were given to do? Because in spite of everything, you take them with Love and Gentleness and Tears?"

Hmm...

"Young man. You are an instrument of peace and justice, and release. A triple-edged sword, perhaps, if such a thing could exist. But you and your kind are truly a gift. Even if very few people see you that way." He smiled his crooked old man smile.

I felt, I don't know, lighter, I guess. At peace within my own skin, maybe. Better than I had in a long time, at any rate. And finally, I'm tired. Time for bed.

"Thank you," I said, preparing to blink away.

"No. Thank you. For all that you've done. All that you suffer. All that you are." he stood up, rather shakily. As his hand grasped the brass handle of the door, he turned and added, "I expect I will be seeing you soon."

I watched until he was safely inside the building. Then I went home for a nap. I hoped, as I closed my eyes, that the old man would be on my list when his time came. I also hoped it wouldn't be any time soon.

That night, I went to my "Shift" in a considerably better frame of mind than I had the night before. Some of the people I met in those brief moments were glad I had come, smiling and peaceful, accepting that it was their time and glad for it. Some not so much; they kicked and screamed and begged. But I took them anyway. As gently as they allowed me to.

It was many weeks later before the old man and I met again. He welcomed me with the same crooked smile as I stood at his bedside, unseen by his friends and family. "I'm ready," he whispered. "It's been a good life.

Smiling myself, I took his hand in mine and gently released him from the mortal remains that imprisoned his spirit. I even stayed long enough to watch him go to whatever awaited him on the other side of the veil.

I hoped the Powers That Be had something good in store for him.

Then I went back to work.

Tale 2: Kip

They call me Kip.

As names go, I suppose Kip isn't too bad. It will do anyway if someone really wants to get my attention. Not that many people even notice me, except to kick me or point disgusted fingers, or call me useless. Some even accuse me of being a drain on the social system.

Like dude!

If I were getting any welfare money, do you seriously think I'd look like this?

Dress like this? It took a while, but I've learned to ignore them. *Mostly*.

Kip isn't my real name. It is the name that's written on the back of the coat I found in a dumpster somewhere and decided was good enough to wear. Especially, in the late fall, like it is now, when the winds are beginning to howl along the streets and frost is coating the windows in the mornings.

Funny. I used to think frost was pretty, the way it made imaginary fronds and star shapes and sparkled in the morning sunlight. But that was back when I had a home with central heating, and food came from refrigerators.

Now it's just the first dance in a long marathon of cold and bleakness and hunger. But I've got my coat and a couple of other layers of cast-offs that keep me toasty. For now, anyway. Which is the only way I can do this. Worry about today. Tomorrow will bring its own problems.

Speaking of problems. Here comes the local "*gangstas*" swaggering down the street in their jeans and matching jackets, gang tats and signs boldly visible. A group of boys with nothing better to do than pick on everybody else. They take great pleasure in making life difficult for people like me. So, I duck into an alley hoping they don't see me. Make myself as small as possible in the corner and hide my face inside my coat. Then I wait. And wait some more because you just never know, right? They could have decided to hang out at the mouth of the alley and make rude noises at the other people walking by.

I wait so long that my legs go numb before I think it's safe to move again. So, I shuffle slowly out of my hiding place, listening for anything other than the usual noise of traffic, car horns and people walking and talking. I'm lucky. The crew has moved on. I'm safe again.

I shuffle down the street, my head down, not looking at anything any higher than the tops of my too-big runners. But I'm hyper-aware of everyone and everything that I meet. Each is a potential threat, and I have someplace to get to. No time for idle chatter. Haha.

By the time I reach the back of the grocery store, the wind has started to pick up again. The tails of my coat are flapping against my legs. The pins and paperclips I use to keep it mostly closed have lost their grip on the cloth. Deal with that later. Right now, I hunker down behind a stack of pallets to wait. The cleaners will be tossing out the no- no-longer-good-enough-to-sell stuff soon. Presently, I am joined by two or three others who, like me, want first pickings.

I wonder if the cleaning people know we are out here waiting. Not that it would change anything if they did probably. They have a job to do and we have needs. In my book that's a win-win situation. I, for one, try not to leave a mess behind when I'm done. But I suppose there are critters besides us that need food too, so anything that gets dropped or left behind probably doesn't go to waste.

Right on schedule, the back door opens and two young guys come out toting a couple of hefty bags each. They talk and laugh with each other as they open the dumpster and toss the bags in. Neither of them looks around before they go back indoors.

We wait a bit, the three of us, to make sure nobody else is coming out that door, then we quietly lift the lid. By tacit agreement, we at least try to act like human beings. No fighting. No arguing. If the first guy scores something good, he shares it with the rest. Otherwise, it's first-come come first-served.

That night, I managed to shuffle away with a package of donuts and an apple, which would do me for breakfast, half a loaf of bread, a few carrots, some pieces of mushy, cut-up fruit that I had to eat there, and a roll of summer sausage. Oh, and joy of joys! A bottle of slightly flat Coke. With no way to cook, it was all carried away and eat stuff. But the gnawing hunger in my belly was at least partly satisfied. My thirst was taken care of. Everything else I would consume when I got to my usual sleeping place.

A decent haul. Maybe enough calories to get me through another night. Assuming that something didn't happen between now and morning. It's twilight when I get to my place. The sidewalks are starting to empty. Or at least as much as they ever do in a city. A drunk is squatting in a puddle of his own mess at the corner between his watering hole and my home. So, I step around him carefully. He could be one of those mean drunks who don't like anybody to see when they are in disarray. Or worse one of the chatty kinds that will unburden all their problems on anybody who looks like their listening. He was busy. So, I got away clean. *What a relief.*

But having him there at the top of the alley created another problem. As much as I wanted to slip into my hidey hole, I didn't dare. Too much chance of somebody seeing. And if someone saw, then I would have to move again. I hate moving. Though in all fairness I was gonna have to soon anyway. It never pays to stay in the same spot for too long. So again, I hunkered down behind some crates to wait.

Naturally, I suppose, since I was more or less secure behind the crates, and had nothing better to do, I started to think and remember. I remembered the child I had been once, laughing and happy sometimes, cranky and miserable at others. But certain that my world was secure and safe no matter what.

I remembered green grass, pets, the smell of freshly-baked bread, the scent of laundry hanging in the house, and the smoky warmth of the old stove. I remembered fresh milk and fresh eggs, and homemade butter. I remembered standing at the window in the dark while a lightning storm raged and counting with my siblings the seconds before the thunder. I remembered mud pies and picking peas, whole wash tubs of them. I remembered music and wiener roasts. I remembered fights, but never what the fight was about.

Until one day, we moved. Just Mom and us kids. And the first blow to my fragile ego when the father that I was so sure loved me, even if I wasn't perfect, never came around again. My young self wondered why. Had I been bad? Had I been unworthy after all? Was it because I wasn't perfect? Why? The question that was never answered.

Then, memory skipped forward a few years. A half-grown child trying to find a way to fit in with peers that had been together for years, but always knowing that I was different, always an outsider, never really part of the clique. Still subject, however, to the same angst and heart-breaking crushes that mark those formative years. The mental wounds gaped wider, but I learned to ignore them. Swallow them. Pretend they weren't there.

Still not worthy.

What do they want? Will they love me if I give them what they want? Another question that was never answered.

So, the butterfly of memory flitted from one brief scene to another. From attempts to make myself something that apparently, I was never to be. Each began with the promise of dawning hope and joy, that I had finally managed to make the right choice. But alas. It seemed that, no matter what I tried, ultimately it was doomed to fail.

Until at last, the creature I am now was born.

Ragged. Shattered. Terrified. Confused. Living from moment to moment because that's all I dared hope for anymore. A being as full of mistrust for other humans as it was full of self-loathing.

Sadly, I drew myself out of the mental wanderings and cautiously surveyed the immediate area. Nothing had changed.

Briefly, I felt a cold shadow. Then the drunk was no longer kneeling. Instead, he was falling over, a husk covered in his own excrement. Death had come a calling. "*Asshole*," I whispered. "You missed me."

Time to go. Before anybody found the body. Or me.

As quickly as I dared, I scuttled out of the alley. I didn't realize that the wind had grown even more in the time I had been hidden. Now it tore at my poor coat like a mad thing. Bits and pieces of typical city flotsam and detritus danced in the eddies of air and tangled about my legs. There was the bite of snow-yet-to-come in its raging maw. Already, my bare hands were aching. But I had to hold the coat closed as best I could against the elemental force, and the sleeves of the coat were too short to bury my hands in and still do that. Gritting my teeth, tucking as much of me as I could inside, I stumbled on.

One street. Two. Cross against the light. A blaring horn and stabbing headlights. But safely across. Check the alley. Nope. No shelter there. No crates. No dumpster. Out of the alley and carry on. Another street. Another alley. *No luck*.

I was getting colder. Slower. More clumsy than usual. My fingertips were numb with cold. My ears burned. My eyes filled with tears as I walked into the wind and the tears froze on my face. I had to find shelter somewhere soon. Or Death really would find me tonight.

At the last of my strength, ready to give in, curl up in a doorway and let come what may, I found what I needed. In an alley between two large stone buildings, I found a pile of garbage bags. And a large cardboard box. Even more fortunate, there was a slight bend in the alley that helped to shear off the worst of the wind.

With numb fingers I felt among the bags, hoping perhaps there would be some softness there. I found a couple that I thought might do and tossed them into the box. Then I took the time to arrange it so the opening wasn't visible and was protected from the wind. Once I was satisfied with that, I piled the rest of the bags against the outside of the box to further disguise it and add more insulation.

I have no idea how long it took to get it all arranged. As cold as I was, it seemed like forever. But finally, I crawled inside. Shivering, I made myself as small as possible on the makeshift bed.

The box rocked a little. But I was fairly sure I'd be safe here. For tonight anyway.

Gradually, the shivering eased up. My head cleared enough that I remembered the treasures in my pocket from the grocery store. Calories that I desperately needed to warm me up again. Hands shaking, I pulled out the bread. Carefully, one slice at a time, I ate it from the middle out by tearing out little pieces to avoid the mouldy parts. I wanted to eat all of it. Really needed to eat all of it. But I didn't dare. I had no idea how far I'd walked tonight, so I had no clue where my next meal would come from. Every few mouthfuls, I sipped the flat Coke.

Regretfully, I put those away, then decided I was too tired to deal with opening the sausage. Like the donuts and the apple, it could wait for morning. I snuggled down into the comfort of the bed, wishing I had thought to grab my blanket from the other place. It was thin and full of holes, but it was better than nothing. *Sigh.*

I dozed off finally. Only to be awoken later when I felt a small furry body curl up next to mine. Terrified, at first, I thought it was a rat. But it was shivering and not trying to bite me or anything, so I reached out a tentative hand. It licked my questing fingers, whined a little, and snuggled closer to me. It was hard to tell in the dark, but it seemed that I had acquired a puppy! Oh well. Warmth was warmth, and it seemed we both needed it. It felt kinda good not to be alone. I think I even smiled a little. So, I tucked him into my midsection, covered us both with the coat, and went back to sleep.

The new day (I can't say morning because I had no idea what time it really was, and it had been a long night) began with wet puppy kisses as my new companion woke me up. In the half light of my new home, I could see that the little critter wasn't really a puppy so much as a really small dog. His fur was so dirty and matted that it was hard to tell what his predominant colour was. But as I stroked him, I could feel just about every bone in his body.

The poor guy wasn't in any better shape than me. "Been out here a while, too, huh?" It had been so long since I'd spoken out loud, my voice came out in a hoarse whisper. "Want some breakfast?" I dug out the package of donuts. He wagged his little nubbin of a tail and smiled a doggy smile at me. But even as hungry as he was, he didn't lunge at the package. "Somebody taught you manners, I see." I inspected the package briefly. From somewhere, I recalled that chocolate wasn't good for dogs, and since I didn't want to make him sick, I gave the contents a look. Nope. We were good. So, I tore off little pieces and we shared the donuts. Then the apple too, after I bit off the bruised parts.

All too soon, the food was done, and it was time to face whatever the new day was going to bring. Having slept curled up in the box, it took me a minute or two to unwind from the cramped position and crawl out.

Staying as hidden as I could, I paused to listen for anything beyond the ordinary, assessing possible threats before I came fully erect. My little friend was not quite so cautious. He bounced out of our shelter and ran to the head of the alley then turned around and ran back. Either he had no sense of self preservation, or there were no threats that he could discern in our neighbourhood.

Trust the pooch? Or trust my instincts? I opted for a middle course. I stood up, stretched a little, adjusted the clothes that had gone askew during the night, and crept among the shadows on the wall toward the opening. My heart was hammering in my chest and pounding in my ears. I breathed with my mouth open, the cool air whistling hoarsely over my tongue. Every muscle in my body was ready to take flight at any moment. But I made it that far. Then I stopped to listen.

The usual traffic noises. But fewer or thinner than I was used to. Was I in a residential district maybe? Maybe I had gone further than I thought the night before and I was actually on the edge of the city?

I peeked around the corner of the brick building then pulled back. The pressure in my chest lightened. My breathing became less frantic.

No huge crowds of people. No signs of gangs or thugs. The buildings that I saw were mostly older brick things, heavy and stately and well-kept by their owners or a maintenance crew. The trees, laid bare by the winds, were all neatly lined up along the walk. A few stubborn flowers still added splashes of colour in window boxes and planters.

I took another, longer, peek. Catty corner to my alley, a small park with swings and slides waited for kids. From the trampled areas in the dying grass, I guessed that there were quite a few who used it. Or a few who used it often. Fortunately for my sanity, not at the moment, though.

"Well, Rennie. It doesn't look like we are in Kansas anymore." I think that's how that movie line went.

Rennie just wagged his almost tail and sat at my feet.

One thing I did know for sure was that neither of us could stay here.

Neighbourhoods like this one took a very dim view of people like me squatting in their back alleys. Most often, calling the cops, afraid that we were there to rob them blind. I had to admit, though, it wasn't totally without reason.

So, which way to go? Back the way I thought I had come? Or maybe take a walk up to the corner and see where that might lead me? I stepped out of the shadows, still undecided, balancing the possibilities in my head. Rennie (it seemed like as good a name as any for the little mutt) took a few steps towards the corner and then checked to see if I was going to come with him or not. I shrugged and followed as nonchalantly as I could. More brick houses. A corner store/gas station. More neatly trimmed lawns and trees. Light traffic. Painted crosswalks. Brightly painted benches. A few other people are out and about doing their business.

As I walked along with the dog, I shoved my hands deeper into my pockets and tucked my chin into my chest. Each step became harder and harder to make as the familiar sadness drew a shroud over me. Once I had dreamed about living this life. A nice secure little house in a nice secure neighbourhood, my own kids playing in the park and riding a school bus, hot meals and warmth and love and laughter. But my grasping fingers could never quite catch that brass ring. Rennie must have known something was wrong. He stopped walking ahead of me and rubbed up against my legs. Either in sympathy or empathy. Whichever, it helped a little. But I had to blink a few times to clear my blurry vision as we trudged along.

Eventually, we came to another corner. This one was marked by a brick concourse and wide cement steps that led up to a portico and double wooden doors. The building itself was massive. Rough stone and brick work, stained glass windows, and heavy oak framing. Had I been in a better frame of mind, I might have appreciated the simplicity and strength conveyed by the architecture. The minute details in the cornices and gables that lightened the sombre stiffness. The sparkle, even in the present low light, of the reds and golds, and greens of the glass. The shiny brass handrails and door handles. All of which spoke of care and attention to detail.

Unable to go on, I sat down on the lowest step, picked up Rennie, hugged him to my chest and rocked back and forth waiting for the strength to carry on. Or be ordered on. Whichever happened first.

I was so lost in my own misery, I didn't hear the massive wooden door above me slide open, didn't know that anyone had joined us until Rennie squirmed and barked inside my coat. There was a clink as a cup was set down on the step. Then whoever it was retreated back up the steps without saying a word.

Slowly, the aroma of chicken soup wormed its way through the wall of misery. I peeked out the corner of my eye, positive that any moment now, someone would come and chase us away. When they didn't, I unwound a little further and slowly reached for the cup. It wasn't hot anymore, but it was still warm, so I took a couple of quick mouthfuls for myself and then offered the rest to Rennie, who sniffed and lapped delicately at the liquid warmth. Like breakfast, it was soon gone. I looked around, wondering what to do with the empty dish. It didn't seem right to just leave it on the step. I had just about screwed up the courage to at least leave it by the door, and was in fact standing up to do just that, when the door opened again.

Jittery now, I set the cup on the step and backed away a few steps, hyper alert again and mentally cursing myself for letting my guard down even for such a short time as I had.

But the woman standing there made no move toward me. Said nothing to me. She just stood there in her slacks and warm sweater, smiling, relaxed.

"Thanks. For the soup." I croaked.

"You're welcome. If we had known that there were two of you, we would have brought more," she tilted her head.

"Are you still hungry? I could make you a sandwich if you like." she offered.

"No. We didn't mean to be any trouble. We'll go now."

"Seems to me that you know more about trouble than I do." She advanced a step. "Come sit. Let me get you some more soup at least."

Was she trying to keep me here? Had she called the cops or the welfare people? Were they even now on their way to pick up the indigent person on her homey little street? Wary now, I looked around and listened carefully for any sign of impending disaster. I was also checking for avenues of escape, if I heard anything. So far, everything seemed the same. She hadn't moved again. Her face held the same soft smile.

I moved a step closer.

"You're like a skittish deer aren't you. Poor thing. Sit. I'll bring more soup." she disappeared inside.

That was my chance to run. But for some reason, the prospect of more soup kept me rooted to the sidewalk. I wasn't going to sit down. But I decided to wait and see what happened. She returned in a few moments with the promised soup in a bigger cup this time and a nice thick sandwich. She paused for a heartbeat on the top step. But when I didn't run away, she came down and set them on the step between us. Then she retreated. "Drink up while it's hot. I'll bring out some water and food for your friend as well." In and then out again with a bowl of water and a plate of something, which she set on the step by her feet.

With a happy bark, the mutt raced up the stairs and started to eat.

I picked up the cup and began, cautiously, to eat as well. The woman stood watch over us until we were almost done. When the great doors opened again and a man's head popped out, I thought for sure this was it. That the trap had been baited and tripped, and any second now, the cops or some other agency would be here to haul me away. Carefully, I set down my cup and plate, not wanting to see them smashed when I made a run for it.

The man said, quietly, "It's ready." Then went back inside. The door closed soundlessly behind him.

"May I show you something?" she asked me from where she stood.

It seemed rude to outright refuse, so I shrugged.

Slowly, carefully, she came down the steps, pausing on each to see if I would stay or run. Though I stayed close, I never let her get close enough to grab me or any of my clothing. Cold weather was coming and I could not afford to lose whatever warmth I had. But she made no move towards me other than walking in my general direction and at the bottom of the steps, led me away from the front of the building and around to an area hidden behind a wrought iron gate.

She wanted me to go in there? Why? Another trap? But curiosity got the better of me. Slowly, I went inside, step by cautious step, keeping her in front of me and hoping that there was no one sneaking around the other way.

What this area may have been intended for when it was first put in, I have no idea. Perhaps a back way in and out of the building in case of fire. There was a door there that led inside. And a big open space with high walls that blocked a lot of the weather. Presently, that open space was occupied by a heavy canvas tent carefully weighted down with cindercrete blocks and large stones.

The woman walked up to the tent and opened the flap so I could see that inside was a small cot with a pillow and a mound of blankets, a tiny folding table and chairs, and a portable stove loaded with coals that were losing their flame and turning a dull red as they began to heat.

"We have this here for people who might need it. It's yours to use tonight if you want," she said gently. "The gate is never locked. You can come and go as you please."

For a moment, I gaped, first at the tent, then at the woman. Without a word, I sprinted back the way we had come, out the gate, and back to where my cardboard box had been.
Sometime in the intervening hours, the city crews had come by. The box and the bags were gone. There was no trace that they, or I, had been there at all.

Night, of course, was coming fast now. With it came fear and cold and indecision. In agony, I paced back and forth, unable to decide what to do. It seemed that even Rennie had deserted me.

Should I?

Was what she said true?

Did I dare?

What if she was lying?

But what if she was telling the truth?

Round and round my thoughts went.

Maybe I could sneak back and take one of the blankets. It would help keep me warm at least. I made it back to the little gate, still expecting it to be locked. It wasn't. I made it to the tent and opened the flap a little to peer inside, and was met by a happy little bark and a fuzzy body with a stubby tail.

Ever cautious, I inspected the tent, tested the cot and pillow for softness, rubbed a blanket against my sore face, and finally decided that it might be alright to sleep here for tonight anyway. Me and my dog.

Warm and safe. For the first time in forever.

For days, I came and went as sneakily as I could. Trying to not be seen and positive that this would all end without any notice. But it never did. And they fed me simple stuff, like soup and sandwiches and clean water. To my starved body it was ambrosia.

It took a long time. But eventually, I started to trust the people that lived and worked in that building. To repay them for their kindness, I made sure that the grounds around the building were as clean as I could make them.

It took an even longer time for them to get me inside and clean up. It was an experience for all of us I think when I relinquished the coat and layers of clothes and scrubbed away the mountain of dirt that was my disguise. When it was done, I felt sort of like the caterpillar who emerged from the cocoon as a butterfly.

It took time to learn to trust other people. Sometimes I still don't.

Slowly and carefully, they helped me rebuild my life. Or led me to people who could help.

The feral half-human creature that I had been still pokes its head up every now and then when a situation comes up. But she goes back to sleep when I say to myself, "I got this!"

Mostly anyway.

Tale 3: Revenge of the Super Hero

Alone, as I stand on the roof of a midsize brick building. The wind blows strongly, heavy with the promise of rain to come. As my long coat streams around me, the thick red and black silk whispers its song as it dances, from left to right, then behind, pressed tight to my black denim pants. Bits and pieces of paper and other things flit around my booted feet, joining in ecstatically until they are driven to a corner and have nowhere else to go. I am glad that I chose to cut my hair short, the silver strands on the crown of my head no more than an inch or two long. Else, it would be a tangled mess in minutes.

In this moment, when the street lights flicker to life offering pools of golden safety to the people who hurry along the cement walks, clutching purses and bags and their own coats close. Buses stop at regular intervals to accept a few of these and spit out a few more, belching fumes that dissipate quickly. Vehicles of all shapes and sizes stream down the road, starting and stopping at the whim of the red and green traffic lights. *Horns honk*. Snatches of music drift in the air. All the little Barbies and Kens are hurrying to their homes or their night jobs or whatever their life demands and needs are.

For a while, I missed it. *The immediacy*. The drive to do and be. To want, have, get, dream, and wish. Then I remember tears, pain, terror, and anger. I push it away with a shiver. I return to the now of the half-life that is mine. I step to the edge and allow myself to fall.

The sidewalk rushes to meet me, or I it. It hardly matters. At the last second, I say a word, and my descent is slowed. I land with a jangle of silver chains from my boots as they strike the hard surface. My teeth click together. My coat settles around me, all black and red swirls with bits of silver here and there.

The people do not see me, nor the demon that lands in their midst. But some ancient instinct forces them to deviate from their path and avoid touching me or walking in my immediate vicinity. It is a relief for all of us. If we were to touch, the resultant information exchange would be catastrophic for the humans and me, both.

At this moment in time, I have no desire to remember that I had been human once.

I straighten my clothes and look around. A familiar figure walks down the street opposite me. His own coat, smoky grey and hanging at his sides, was untroubled by the wind that whistles down the street and swirls around corners. Intent on his own mission, he stalks along, staying in that no man's land between the light and the dark. He weaves through the foot traffic on the sidewalk, polite as always, avoiding contact as much as he can. Those pedestrians that he can not avoid pass through his thin frame, most not noticing they just walked through a force of nature. Very few will pause and look around before they hurry on their way. Being in the presence of Death has that effect sometimes.

In any case, it appears that he and I will not be working in tandem tonight. A slow night for me then. With a sigh, I turn in the opposite direction and begin walking. I open my special sense and listen for the word that calls me: *revenge*.

Every person on the planet, no matter how mild-mannered they appear to be, carries that dark seed in the core of their being. Ninety-nine percent will never act on it. Or if they do, it is a petty, weak thing easily managed without help from an outside source. They write a letter, start a rumour, wound but do not kill, instances that ultimately do more damage to their own psyche than to the object of their anger.

It is the other one percent that I am interested in. The man, the woman, occasionally the child, who is so damaged by the depravity of another and has no recourse and no rest from their personal nightmare. In the vaults of their mind, they call out to me. Their own personal vigilante. A force of human nature made incarnate by the strength of the desire and need of the caller.

Generally, my actions lead to the perp being caught by the authorities. Or sometimes the creation of a physical and/or mental breakdown that leaves them in much the same condition as their victims. Not every stroke, tumour, disease, or mental break is my fault. Sometimes people get sick just because (ask the Powers That Be why, not me).

Sometimes, though, revenge involves Death.

In fact, that is how this all got started in the first place:

Once I had been a human child. Small for my age with fly-away white blonde hair. Like all children, I played with toys, read comic books, and basked in the praise of the adults in my world; "Oh, she is so pretty. She looks like a little *China Doll*. She's eight? Really? She's so tiny she looks like she's only five!".

Even though we lived in a poor part of the city, I felt safe because all of our neighbours made a point of looking out for me. Especially because my mother spent a lot of time "working" at night. We didn't have a lot. But it was enough, I suppose. Then one night, she came home with Floyd. He was a big guy. Built all square and solid like a walking apartment building. His voice was deep and rough-sounding. At first, I think because he was so large, he scared me. But mother seemed to like him. They spent a lot of time in the bedroom making noise anyway.

For a while, things got better. He bought both of "*his girls*" nice things to wear. The heat was turned on again. We had food on the table. We drove to places instead of walking or taking the bus. It was great. We were happy. I thought we would stay that way. I still don't know what happened. But one night, Floyd came home in a towering rage. He yelled at his mother. He broke things. He slapped her hard enough to make her nose bleed. I was terrified. So, I hid until he stormed out of the apartment.

But after that, things got really ugly really fast in my world. Hardly a day went by that Floyd didn't slap mother for something. I tried to be quiet when he was there. Mostly I hid, reading my comic books to tune it out. I was glad I was small. I could squish myself into tiny corners when I had to. Then one really bad night, Mother fought back when Floyd hit her. She came after him with a butcher knife. They struggled briefly. But it was no good. Floyd was just so huge and strong. He took the knife away from her. I heard the cracking sound as the bones in her arm broke. I saw her fall to the floor and Floyd kneeling over her screaming mean words as he stabbed her. Mother screamed once. Then she was silent. Blood was everywhere. Floyd slammed out of the apartment. He still had the knife and he was splattered with bright red.

I came out of my hiding spot, my white nightgown twisting around my legs. I had to see if she was okay. I got blood all over me, the smell thick and metallic and sweet. "Mama! Mama!" I sobbed and cried as I knelt there. She was still breathing. But it was thin and raspy sounding. I knew I had to get help. But in my panic, instead of knocking on the neighbours' doors I ran out the back door of the building. And ran smack into Floyd. I remember trying to run away and him chasing me and grabbing my hair. After that things are pretty much a blur except for one small burning pain in my chest.

The next thing I remember is being someplace sort of silvery grey with no real light and no sound at all. That and a need to get help for my mother before Floyd went back to the apartment. So instead of going "forward", I went "back". I saw the policemen, the ambulance guys and a crowd of people all standing around staring at the alley and each other. A neighbour that I recognized was talking to one of the policemen, pointing at our building and waving her arms like crazy. Finally, he and an ambulance man/paramedic went with her inside. I stood and watched with everyone else but nobody talked to me or pushed me out of the way. It was like I wasn't there. I had to listen really hard to hear what they were saying. "The poor kid. Used to see her sometimes with her mamma. What was her name again? Melody or something like that I think."

"Melody? My name is Melody. I 'm the only Melody around here!" I said.

I think I even jumped up and down and tried to grab the lady's sweater. Not surprising, my hand went right through it and she shuddered like something cold had touched her. Okay that was creepy.

In a daze, or just plain stunned, I stood at the corner of the building and watched some more. More ambulances came and more policemen. They brought mamma out on a rolly bed. She had tubes stuck in her and a mask on her face. But she was safe now and that was good. They went away with sirens blaring. Then the police started taking a look in the alley and leaving little yellow and green card things everywhere around two lumps covered with blankets; a great big one and a little one.

I think that was when I finally figured it all out. Or started anyway. Little ghost me hung around the apartment building for a long time. Mostly just watching and trying to think about what I was supposed to do now. I learned a few tricks too. Some on purpose. Some by accident. Like listening to people's thoughts instead of just their words. I sort of remembered some of my favourite comic book heroes that could do that. So, I called it my *"super power"*.

I was still there when mamma came home from the hospital. I heard her thinking about a funeral, mine presumably, and "that she was glad that the cop had shot Floyd dead. It was the only revenge she was going to get for losing her baby and being all scarred up from the knife. How was she supposed to work with scars like those? Who wanted a hooker with big red knife scars?"

Then she cried for a long time and I tried to make her feel better. But she didn't know I was there so it didn't work. The last time I saw her was at my funeral. There were a lot of people there. They all looked sad and cried a lot and thought about how brave my mother was sitting there all by herself beside the casket. The preacher said a bunch of words about love and death and forgiveness and revenge being the province of the Almighty.

There was that word again!

I quit listening and started to think about that word and what it meant. I was still sitting in the church thinking when the people were gone and the flowers and the smell of perfume were all that was left. So little ghost me left the church and wandered around randomly listening for the word revenge in other people's thoughts and comparing that to the wisdom of my comic book heroes, who all started out as someone looking for revenge against the bad guys.

The first thing I decided was that, in order to be a superhero I needed to look the part. So, I grew up. Quicker than I would have alive, but it was still a process that took time and made me tired. I spent my down time either in the library (because doors and windows meant nothing anymore) reading. I found out that if I ran my hand over a book, I could pretty much see every word. So as the body grew so did the mind. I quit thinking like an eight-year-old and became the adult that I appeared to be. Psychology texts were of particular interest. I still think Sigmund Freud was pretty screwed up. *But whatever.*

Next of course, once I was done growing, was the right clothes. Even if nobody could really see me, I figured I might as well look the part. You know. Just in case. So, I wandered through clothing stores trying on different looks. In a motorcycle shop I found my boots; black leather, snub nosed, low heeled with silver chains around the boot that jingled pleasantly when I walked in them. In a Walmart I found the black jeans that fit snugly and flared a little at the knee for my boots. In a second-hand store I found my black tee with the words "*Bad Girl*" in sparkly red vinyl on the front. The hardest thing to find was my coat. In the end I picked a style that I liked (something called a duster) and recreated it in heavy black silk with red and silver swirls. The only bling I chose was a belt for my jeans in silver and sparkly crystals.

So. All grown up and tricked out in my "costume", I went back to the streets to hunt for the evil-doer. I started small with petty thieves who had a favourite habit of stealing little old ladies' purses on check day. Most of them were either looking for money to get high, or they were already high and looking for a thrill. For the little old ladies, their revenge was invariably that the thieves be caught or find out what it was like to be at the mercy of little thugs like them. *Easy peasey*. Done.

Then one day, I ended up in my old--haunt--(haha)-as another group of idiots were robbing a little old lady. She was fighting valiantly, but just like with my mother and Floyd, there was no way she would win. And just like little me, there was nothing I could possibly do to help.

"Stupid old bitch! Shoulda minded yer own fuckin' bizness. But nah. Just couldn't leave it go could ya." one thug snarled as he viciously kicked her in the ribs. When they left a few minutes later, their victim was barely recognizable. Her face was a mass of pulped flesh and blood oozed everywhere. She almost certainly had broken ribs and her left arm lay on the concrete at an odd angle. Her mind was a red haze of pain so bad that try as I might, I could not get past it to see the rest of the story. But somehow, she was clinging to life.

For now, at any rate as Death was nowhere in sight, "Hmm. So, this was about more than a simple robbery." I thought as I followed the thugs—which was not hard as they left a trail of the old lady's stuff behind them. The trail finally ended at an old building that may have been a garage at one time but had long since been boarded up and abandoned. They were inside, busily congratulating each other on their accomplishment and what sort of "reward" they were likely to get from Sly for eliminating the "*problem*" for him.

So. My first step obviously was to make certain that the police were able to track these guys as easily as I did. Preferably before they ditched their bloody clothes and made-up alibis.

Not quite so easy peasey. But I managed to keep the trail from moving and then directed the cop's attention to it by forcing him to move away from me until he was almost right on top of it.

Revenge 1. Thugs 0.

My second step was to make certain (if I could find a way) that the victim stayed alive long enough to at least tell the cops her story. So, after a little searching, I finally found the right hospital and pretty much camped out by her door to stop Death from coming in until she was able to talk. Strangely, he walked by a few times. Even nodded to me once. But that was all.

Revenge 2. Old Lady 1. Thugs (and Sly) 0.

The final step was learning as much about this Sly person as possible and seeing what I could do to rock his world. For a while it was just small annoyances that, amazingly, involved the three thugs A LOT. When he'd finally had enough and decided eliminating them was a good business decision I was there. So was the other guy.

Revenge 3. Old Lady 2. Sly 0. Thugs -3.

As we were walking away, D asked, "Don't feel sorry for them at all do you?"

I considered it for a second. "Nope. What they get they've earned one way or another." Then I added, "It will be Sly's turn sooner or later too. Pretty sure the world won't miss any of them for too long."

There wasn't much he could say to that. So, he just nodded and went back to work.

I just wandered down the road, heading back to familiar territory. Thinking.

Should I feel bad for the way everything has played out? Has there been a better way to deal with it?

After all, the old lady had died from her beating. So, dying in their turn was justified. And their deaths would, I hope, lead to justice for Sly and the rest of his cronies (if the clues that I was incidentally leaving worked). Okay. *Universal balance sustained.*

Unfortunately, as I ambled away, a few niggling doubts wormed their way into my head. What if?

What about?

Could I?

Should I?

GAH! My super hero friends never had to think about this stuff!

Eventually, I decided that I could be more selective in my clientele. So petty things (the letters and rumour group) could figure out their own stuff. I would concentrate my attention on the bigger things, and maybe, try not to get anyone killed along the way (sorry D, it's been fun but you know...).

So, another slow night. D goes his way. I go mine. Both doing our bit for the world at large. I'm glad.

"Vengeance is Mine." sayeth the Lord. Or something like that.

I am pretty sure that I am sort of a sub-contractor for the PTB.

Hmm. Wonder what it would take to get a raise?

Tale 4: We, The Powers

Known by many names, in many languages, by many peoples, we are the Powers That Be. Universally hated, loved, revered, detested, ignored, blamed, sworn by, sworn on, and sworn at. We are ancient beyond imagination and, to be honest, we are not even sure how we came to be, nor where we will be in the eons to come. We are many, yet also so few. We are powerful. We like to think we are wise. We, my sisters and brothers and I, have watched over this blue marble in the cosmos for so long that it's almost become a habit.

Yes. We are many things. But there are many things we are not as well.

We are not omnipotent. For if we were there would be no need for free will, which is the guiding force that directs even such as we. Every decision made by man, woman, or child on Earth, and the consequences for the choice, rest with that person. We can only guide and sometimes, when they listen carefully, show them the possible results.

We are not omniscient. Even if we do not know all the possible results of all the possible choices of every single person. To be able to do so would surely drive us mad. Which is not to say that humans in general do not send us to the brink of sanity occasionally. But, so far, we are still as sane as we ever were, and the world spins on.

We are not omnipresent. Again, down that road lies insanity. At one time, when there were only a few thousand here and there, we were more hands-on. But once the population grew to hundreds of millions, we had to find a better solution and still let our people feel that we were there. So, we mostly concern ourselves with particular points in time and areas and people, whose choices may have far-reaching effects on the world. For the rest, we try to spend a little time each day with each one of you and enlist the aid of those you call Guardian Angels or Guiding Spirits who know the general basics of the paths you are likely to take. They come to us if there is a deviation that needs attention or a concern of some sort.

They keep us informed, pass on information, as well as directions. *When you choose to listen.* and you feel your needs are being listened to at least. It isn't a perfect system by any means.

But it's worked so far. We are a family of sorts. Like a family, we do not always agree on everything. In fact, there are one or two who are diametrically opposed to just about every decision the rest of us ever make. It is frustrating beyond belief. But in its own way, it keeps us... honest, and, again, offers a different choice to the lives we affect.

We are, as stated, powerful in our own ways, and because of that, we cannot act directly upon the Earth herself or the lives within it. To do so would invite disaster for all living things and might, possibly, be the end of the Earth as we, and you, know it. Therefore, works and tasks are performed by various entities, mostly unseen, who do as we bid them do. Often, their duties are onerous and unpleasant, and they are on the receiving end of the blame game that people are so fond of. At least at first. In my experience, that soon evolves to include us rather swiftly.

We have grown used to it, of course. Of necessity, we have grown very thick skins. But do not ever make the mistake of thinking that we enjoy causing pain. It is, however a wonderful catalyst for change. How and why, where and when the change takes effect, is a function of the free will I mentioned previously.

Certainly not all are unseen and hidden. Over the millennia, we have used Prophets, Seers, and Fortune Tellers to express our messages. The results have been mixed. Oftentimes, the said person was considered insane or a liar. Or, even worse, the message is so garbled or misunderstood that it is no longer causing the desired effect. The unfortunate tool is then disposed of, usually in a gruesome and very public manner. But the mangled message lives on to become even more misunderstood. Often, the results are disastrous.

A very few seers and sensitives do manage to survive and spread the truths they are given. Slowly, they spread the word. One person at a time, they make minute changes in the understanding of those around them. It is a slow way to create change.

Change only happens quickly in the aftermath of war or disaster. It is a wonderful catalyst for bringing out the best- and the worst- in people. I know we are not supposed to but as my thoughts move on, I find myself returning often to three particular agents at my disposal. Something about these three and the lives they touch reminds me of life before we grew so thick-skinned.

Not so very long ago, one of my particular agents was offended by the fact that he had been given a list that included a number of babies. It seemed to him that there were an inordinate number of such lists given to him. So offended, or wounded, was he that he considered quitting.

Now, in truth, I can not say I blame him for feeling this way. It is one of the more difficult tasks given to such as he. So small. So, innocent. So, trusting.

To end before you've barely begun. Surely there is a better solution?

But is there?

Would it be better to live and die as Melody did, shot or very nearly stabbed to death, by a crazed brute of a man?

Or perhaps in the house fire that may take the parents at a later date?

Do those endings seem more kind?

Of course, not every one of them would eventually end in a horrific manner. Some would live their lives, quietly and carefully, die quietly and carefully, and in the end wonder if they had ever lived at all....

Why did they or do they have to end at all? Sadly, it is not an answer that I can give without spending a millennium explaining the delicate balance that we try so very hard to maintain between the possibilities that we know of. I suppose the shortest answer is that everything must end so that something else can begin.

Do I expect you to just accept that answer?

Honestly? No.

It isn't in your nature to accept without questioning. It's one of the more frustrating and fascinating things about the way the mind works. It's also what led to some marvelous discoveries over the years. And gives me endless migraines occasionally.

In any case, through the good agency of another of my kindred, he was shown the basic truths of the matter and resumed his work. *I was pleased.* He is, in fact, one of the best ones that I have to work with. He does not remember of course, but he was not always my agent. He was a normal flesh and blood human once. Who lost his entire family to a virulent plague that swept the world, before ingenuity and necessity taught people how to combat that particular disease. Or build immunities to it that were effective.

When, after yet another catastrophe, his life also ended, he was given a choice. Go on to whatever lies next, or become an agent for US. He chose Us obviously and, because he also chooses to be this way, he does his job as best he can, as smoothly as he can, as cleanly as he can and as swiftly as he can. Not all are as careful as he is. *Which is a pity*. But again, choices.

Strangely, they seem to be everywhere. Act and react however you choose. But be ready to accept the consequences. And know that soon there will be yet another choice looming in the near distance.

Melody Anita Rose Yarrow is another of our unseen agents. She was also once a real girl. Who died swiftly at the hands of my other. What she became on her death was accidental, because she was not supposed to return. We are still working out what she is likely to become: loose cannon of the Spirit World or Avenger of wrongs? Since she is an unknown and new entity in the Perpetual Chess game, like the Queen, she moves where she pleases, sometimes guided by her friend/cohort, Death. Together, they are a strange pairing. Perhaps because she is so young, she reminds him of his own children. Perhaps he feels a responsibility for her.

In any case, we will have to see where it leads, if it leads anywhere. Who knows, she may even get a raise. And then there is Kip. *Wounded. Broken. Young. Wise. Caring. Strong. Determined*. Able to glimpse Death when he is near. Braver than even she realizes.

From her could come many paths into darkness and into light.

Perhaps that is why I find her endlessly fascinating.

Now, having given a few of you a brief glimpse into the Celestial, I will return to the halls between the stars and see what may lie next upon the marvellously fascinating marble called Earth.

****

Well, gee whiz! Wasn't that enlightening? I'll bet you ALL feel so much better now.

Pfft. Pompous ass, isn't he? Do you really care how we think and why we do what we do?

Be honest now.

Didn't think so.

All you really care about is yourselves. And the dirt you stand on.

Well, let me tell you a little secret:

Yes, I am *"diametrically opposed"* to most of the little changes that he is doing.

Why?

In the beginning, I found you as interesting as he did and apparently, still does.

But as the eons moved on, I watched you consistently make the choices that led to war, murder, and the destruction of everything that you were supposed to care about. You walk. You talk. You think. But in the deepest darkest parts of your minds, you aren't any better than the apes that you used to be.

Yeah ok. War has its uses. But why do you always have to start with a bigger, better weapon instead of going directly to "Hey! Can we talk about this?"

In my view, you were an experiment that's gone horribly wrong. If it were my choice, I'd let you have at it, get it over with, wipe the Earth clean and start all over.

But even I am stuck on that whole free will clause in the ancient contract.

So, what he builds, I tear down.

I am that other little voice in the darkness. And some day, who knows, I might get my wish.

****

Tsk. Tsk. They are how old and they still refuse to grow up! Boys!!! Argh!!

I'm going for a nap. Wake me if anything interesting happens. And by anything, I mean something not done by Builder Boy or Mr. Death to All.

****

Though it pains me to say this, both of my brothers have valid points.

As a species, people are truly fascinating and complex. Cruel and yet kind, equally capable of truth and falsehood, they hurt and they heal, naive and wise, capable of wonder and certain of their knowledge. So full of love and hate.

Each and every one is a walking, talking contradiction.

Which is why I seldom support my brother in his scheme to wipe it all out and begin again.

Nor can I see what may lie beyond so drastic a step as that. Utter chaos? The end of Us, perhaps?

I fear that, should we lose our devotees, then we too shall diminish and be as nothing in the spaces between the stars. A fate I am not prepared to accept for myself or my kindred.

****

You know what?

I like words.

People have come up with some truly amazing words over time.

Like entropy; disenfranchisement; devastation; ruination; calamity.

Perhaps some day, I shall write a poem with these words.

****

LALALALALALALA!!!!

****

Have you ever had a family member who drives you to the brink of insanity? I did not think it was possible that this could happen to me. But apparently, even such as we are not exempt from such thoughts and desires. All I want to do is have a little fun with those pitiful human creatures. You know, throw them curveballs and watch them scurry around like rats in a maze after non-existent cheese.

Of late, however, my simple little pleasures in life seem to be redirected by the advent of one (or possibly more) of my family members. The frustration alone is enough to make me want to blow something (or perhaps someone) up.

Try as I might, very few of my attempts to create chaos have culminated in the desired effect. I think the last time that came close was during some little skirmish of theirs they called *WW2*. But every time I get close, some idiotic little goodie goodie progressive steps in and ultimately turns everything to sunshine and butterflies.

I hate butterflies! And horrible, wholesome sunshine....

I think I'm gonna go blow up a volcano or something......

Grrrrr...................

****

And of the others, there lies only silence......................

Tale 5: Showdown

With the ease of practice and familiarity, I stalk and pace the streets and alleyways, tents and tenements, clapboard houses, brick and mortar buildings, hallways, bedrooms, offices, dens, playgrounds, and backyards. All are within my purview. It doesn't matter who you are or where you are. I will, eventually, come to you. It's my responsibility. I always keep my appointments.

Money can't hide you. Begging doesn't stop me. Pity, and my personal code of ethics will affect how quickly I do my job. Regardless, the job gets done.

What happens when I'm done? I guess that's up to you and the PTB. Above my pay grade. No need to know. I like it that way. This job is complicated enough for a simple guy like me.

Whenever possible, on my nightly tour, I try to save the hospital for last. When there aren't a lot of people around, the antiseptic halls are soothingly quiet. I like it best that way when I visit someone's loved one.

I'm almost always the only "other" being there. Once in a while though, I see Melody, dressed in her "*Bad girl*" outfit, standing by the bed of someone, listening to the words of their inner heart: a sparkly, pale, shadow of the middle dark, eyes intent as she focuses, sometimes, but not always, touching the sheet wrapped figure on the bed.

Every time I see that girl, it sparks a strange feeling in my gut.

I remember, vividly, the day she became whatever the hell she is. I was the one who crossed her over. Except she didn't completely cross and came back. Same little girl. But in a teenage body. Weird.

I'm not sure how she managed to do either one of those things. I puzzle over it at odd moments.

Wonder if it's ever happened before. Or if it will happen again. Or why the PTB let it happen at all. Which means it's also above my pay grade and best just keep out of it..

I do my damnedest to live by the *KISS* method. Keep. It. Simple. *Stupid.*

My long-gone wife would have called me a neanderthal.

So anyway, this one night I'm schlepping my butt casually down the hospital corridor, appointment list complete. Out of the corner of my eye, I see Melody standing over a guy in a white lab coat. Poor guy is almost curled up in the fetal position on the cold floor. Obviously, he's bawling or trying to stop himself from doing it. Melody is just standing there, watching him, her head tilted a little. Sort of like an owl.

Business as usual.

"Hey kid," I say, tipping my imaginary hat in her general direction.

Ok. So, I don't often talk to her-or anyone really-because I don't want to intrude on a rather intimate moment. But it's not like we've never talked. She's thrown some business my way. So, the way I see it, we are confederates in this crap shoot called half life.

So, she turns her head and looks at me. Her big eyes get bigger, and her face, pale anyway, gets whiter, almost luminescent.

The look she gave me gave me the creeps. Chicken skin and everything.

Macho me booked it outta there as fast as I could go.

The following days were inordinately busy. A cold snap blanketed the city in snow, wind, and ice. Between the car accidents and the homeless who froze where they slept, my job became more about speed than finesse. The PTB weren't listening particularly to anybody's pleas for mercy from the uncommonly low temps. But then, they never really seem to sometimes. Of course, then there are other times when it's the opposite. Sometimes I swear that either it's one guy with bipolar disorder having manic episodes, or they periodically switch who's at the controls. Either way, it sure keeps me hopping.

Even as busy as I was, once in a while, I would catch a glimpse of Melody out of the corner of my eye. Sometimes she would just casually stop in the glow of a street lamp. Sometimes I would get the feeling that she was skulking around the corner watching me. I have no idea what was going on inside her head, or what she wanted or needed from me. It was beginning to creep me out. And annoy me at the same time.

But I was busy enough that I couldn't take the time to deal with whatever her problem was. So, I had to let her little cat and mouse game continue.

I was hoping it was just boredom.

***

So, I was Business as usual, wandering through various places in the city. You know, looking for somebody who needed some specialized help. But all I got were the usual, boring mean girls being stupid about some other girls' clothes or whatever. A store owner here and there was pissed at the competition. You know, nothing interesting. One guy was mad because he was being shaken down (whatever that means) by another lowlife. Thought about it for a sec, remembered the thugs from, like, ages ago, decided not to get involved. Too much hassle.

So, I went to the roof of my building to sit and ponder the big questions of my world. You know, like, are there enough sparkles on my coat? Would my boots look better with a few scuff marks? Would the PTB ever give me a raise? Who was smarter, Einstein or Newton? What does relativity even mean? Was Freud a closet homo? You know, stuff.

So, I'm sitting there, feet dangling over the edge, thinking, and incidentally watching all the goings on below me. Nothing too fantastic. D on his appointed rounds, weaving through the hookers and derelicts, businessmen and vendors. I've always wondered why he does that. I mean, the dude can walk through walls if he wants, but he avoids contact with live people when he's working. And it looked like it was the end of his shift and he was on his way to the hospital for the last bit. He's predictable that way.

I haven't been to the hospital for a while. Mostly, it just depresses me. But I had nothing better to do, so I took the shortcut over the rooftops and got there ahead of him.

As usual, it was quiet except for the whir of machines and canned air, the swish of uniforms, the soft patter of rubber-soled shoes on polished concrete.

I wondered where D was headed. I hoped it wouldn't be the nursery tonight, because I know he hates going there.

So, I'm standing in the middle of the foyer when I hear it. *My personal catnip*. Loud and strong and holy, wow, whoever this was, he was pretty angry.

The guy was in a white doctor's coat, bits of equipment hanging out of pockets. Tears were leaking from his eyes and dripping off his chin. He was young. New to the whole medical scene. But the tears weren't because he was sad. Oh no. This guy was mad as mad gets before it turns to insanity. And who was he mad at? Who did he hate above all others? Who did he want to take revenge on?

Death.

And as luck would have it, who should walk by at that exact second? The Man himself.

The existential possibilities and ramifications of randomness and purpose kind of sent me into a tailspin, so when I looked over and he said, *"Hi,"* it was all just too weird.

I got outta there as fast as I could.

I spent the next couple of days on my rooftop, walking back and forth. Thinking. Trying not to think. But I just couldn't shake the need to act. And believe me, I tried. But the young doc's voice kept crawling into my head, demanding that I do something about his deepest desire. The guy was dead serious when he was thinking about how to get revenge on death. It was an all-consuming passion in his mind. So, I had to take him seriously. Right?

So, I took to following D on his rounds.

Trying to decide what to do. Or not do.

I knew that D knew that something was up. But I couldn't just walk up to the guy and say, "Hey! You remember that doc you saw me with at the hospital? Well, he really hates you. Wants me to avenge him for, you know, doing your job. Sorry dude. Nothing personal. Just business." Can you imagine how well THAT would go over?

Not just with D either...

Damned if you do, damned if you don't.

****

The cold weather finally ended and I was able to get back to my twisted version of normal. Melody was still following me around, but as long as that was all she was doing I supposed I could live with it, so to speak. I would have to find out what was going on eventually. Or wait for her to try something. In the meantime, I had work to do.

A few nights later, a really odd thing happened: I started my shift as usual, but there was no list for me that night....

You have no idea how strange that was. I mean, sure, we have nights when it's slow, only a few people who have their numbers called. But never a night when there was nobody. Anywhere. At least not in my district. Oddly, it was not a comfortable situation for me. It made me restless and more than a little out of sorts. Had the PTB decided to take a holiday and forgotten to forward the memo? Had they switched again, and the new guy had dropped the ball?

As I wandered around, I could hear the pitiful moans of a few who would have welcomed a visit, their pain, mental and physical, thick in the air around them. But I didn't dare do what they wanted. I have no idea what kind of chaos that would create.

As I wandered, perplexed and puzzled by this lack of purpose, I found myself standing at the head of an alley that I was familiar with. The signs of that long-ago night were erased by time and grime. But I remembered it like it was yesterday. The soft feel of her little life in the palm of my hand. The smile as I pulled her out and away so that she wouldn't feel the pain any longer than necessary. The little fingers slipping through mine as she left to become.....

"Hey, D. What brings you here tonight?" from somewhere behind me.

And there she stood in all her finery. The slightly grown version of that sweet, soft little kid who left a mark on me that I couldn't shake. "Hey yourself, Melody." I looked at her side eyes. She seemed a little twitchy standing there. Nervous. Not like her at all.

"Somebody in need here tonight?" Her fingers were picking at the sparkly bits on her cuffs.

"Nope. Just passing by. Stopped for a sec." I turned and leaned against the wall, crossed my arms, and crossed my ankles, looking as casual as I could.

"Oh. Um." She couldn't look me in the eyes.

Wait her out, or ask outright? Assuming she would tell me that is.

"Been seeing you around a lot lately. Got something going on?" Tilt the head, smile. "Anything you need help with?"

"No. Not.... really." She looks down at the pavement, scuffs the toe of one boot against a crack there. "Just...." Heavy pause.

"You look a little. confused. Sometimes it helps if you talk about it." I hoped she'd take me up on the offer.

I sort of hoped she wouldn't. Because I didn't want to get involved in her shenanigans if I could help it. For a second, she looked up at me. Then back at the toes of her boots. She fidgeted around, but I noticed that she didn't try to run away either. So, I leaned against the building and waited.

"It's just that...." she mumbled. "Ah geez. This is just so stupid!" she stomped away.

But not far, and stomped back to me.

"See the thing is...." pause, swallow, gather herself back together, "You know the other night? When you see me at the hospital?" I nodded and shrugged.

And waited. "You know what I do, right? What am I? I wish sometimes they had picked.... *Gah*!" she paced away, little hands fisted inside her coat sleeves. Then paced back. Drew in a big breath and blurted, "The doc I was with wants me to get his revenge! *On YOU*!!

And I don't know what to friggin' do!! It's all just so hard to figure out!!"

My first reaction (which I fortunately did not give in to) was to laugh. She was dead serious and thrumming with indecision and confusion. Besides, at this point, I had no idea what she was really capable of. So instead, I gathered my wits and said, "Oh."

"That's it? That's all you got for me? OH? No profound and pithy sayings? No ancient wisdom?" she shook her head in disgust.

"Well, in my line of work, it really isn't that uncommon, you know. I/We get blamed a lot. For stuff that we can't choose. Fine print in the contract, I guess. But see, the thing is, most people don't really want revenge in the way you are thinking. Not even doctors. What they want is to put me out of business. Eventually, they will realize that doesn't work either. And besides, have you ever met anybody who wanted to live forever?"

"But he was so.... certain that's what he wanted!! Kept repeating it over and over to himself..."

"Well, people are funny. In the heat of the moment, they will think and say and do things that they didn't mean. Or would regret sooner than later." I tried to sound assuring, or at least sure of what I was telling her. I hope I wasn't gonna regret this, but I suggested that we go back to the hospital and check in on the doc. "It seems that, for tonight anyway, I have nothing but time. Shall we?"

So, we strolled down the streets, the pair of us. Two entities with nothing better to do. Just a normal thing to do. We stayed in the shadows as much as possible. We avoided contact with the living. We thought our own thoughts as we walked, silent but companionable.

For a while, anyway.

"We?" she asked, out of nowhere. "Before you said, we. Who's we?"

"Well, believe it or not, there are a lot of us. Each has a district. Each has a shift. This one is mine. I'm the night-time custodian here. But there's someone else who takes over at the end of my shift."

"Huh. Who knew. I always thought it was just you. You guys all seem to look the same to me," and then the light bulb came on. "So, it may not even have been you he was mad at? I've been following the wrong guy all this time?" She looked a little shocked.

"Well, not necessarily. Depends on whether it was one person in particular or a whole bunch over time. Doctors get a little strange when they lose a bunch of patients. Especially the new guys." Then, I suppose because it was in the back of my mind, I had to ask, "So, how would you have got revenge anyway?"

She just looked at me and smiled that secret smile that I used to hate back in the day, and kept on walking.

Shoulda known better...

Oh well. We were at the hospital now anyway.

***

Well, damn and blast!! That was NOT how that was supposed to play out!!

Shit!

Tale 6: The Story of John Jacob.....

It is warm here. The heat of the sunshine on my face is pleasant and soothing. Somewhere nearby, I hear birds twittering in the trees. I wish I could see them. But those days are long past. A fact that I accepted long ago. There have been compensations, though. So, it's alright.

People walk by me as I sit here on the steps of my home, the great oak doors open wide to catch any breeze that may flow through. I smile and nod as they go by. Those who know me will say, "*Good morning, John.*" Those who don't will either frown or nod, or shake their heads at the doddering old man sitting on the steps, basking in the sun. I smile in spite of them and enjoy my day.

Somewhere down the street is a daycare. I hear the children outside playing regularly. I also hear them singing, at the top of their voices, a song that I love and hate in equal measure.

Would you like to know why?

It started out innocently enough with my birth in the middle of the great depression, first son of German immigrant parents. My father, in honouring his forebearers, affixed the name John Jacob to my already simplistic Schmidt. All well and good. Until I started school, one of my teachers, having a more than passing fondness for Vaudevillian musicals, taught us the words to a song: "*John Jacob Guggenheimer Schmidt.....*" whereupon one brilliant classmate went "Hey wait a minute! Isn't that your name? Except for the Guggenheimer part?" And so it began. Children, being casually cruel creatures, tormented me daily with that song after that. It was a very-trying time in my young life.

A time that could have turned me into either a bully. Or a whipping boy. But in fact did neither.

Thank you, Father Francis and Mother, for getting me through those first eight years or so. After that they just called me John. I suppose because by that time we were all too old to be singing it..

In any case, I managed to get through it and high school as well, and went immediately to seminary college after graduation. Much to my mother's delight, after six long years, I walked out of that great stone edifice an ordained priest with the fire of conviction in my heart, certain of my future and strong in my beliefs. Off I went to convert the heathen!

Ah the hubris of youth!!

Which by the way, my aging mother did not find joyful as she had kept the secret hope that I would immediately become the parish priest and she could feed me daily. My father was a lot more understanding. He wanted me to see the world but not down the blue steel lens of a rifle barrel as he had for a short time.

My first posting was in India. Land of *Vishnu, Krishna, Kali, Shiva and Allah*. Of *cobras, cholera, leprosy, malaria* and *innumerable insects*. Of *squalor* and *riches*. Of *misery* and *joy* (you really have to see the Holi celebration of colour to understand). I spent my days in hospitals and hospices ministering medicine and comfort to the sick and dying. I spent the nights offering food and the love of my God to the people in the streets. And I watched the various celebrations and listened to the music. And in spite of myself and the poverty around me, I fell in love with the people.

Did they love me back? I can't really say for certain. But they tolerated me. Even when I started asking questions about their various religions and deities, theological systems, and compared them to my own.

How many did I manage to convert? Actually none. A fact made evident when the great Ganges River flooded, and the people all went to their temples to pray at the feet of their statues and speak to their gods and goddesses. Perhaps, for my sake, because I was trying so hard, they came to my services on Sunday, to nod and clap and sing praises and listen. But when the going got tough? The wise went back to what they knew best and trusted most.

When the time came to depart bright India for my next posting, I chose the route via Vatican City. Perhaps hoping that, what part of my conviction I had lost, I might regain there. Certainly, it was opulent. Obscenely, so after the backstreets of Delhi. But the Hindus also had statues coated in gold leaf and precious gems. So, I looked beyond the bright trappings and saw, in their hearts, most of the people of Rome were equally as happy. The only real difference was the circumstances of everyday life and health. It seemed to me in the years that followed, the same could be said for most of the places I was posted at. Living conditions were less than ideal. But the people themselves were at peace with their place in the world, trusting their environment and their gods to give them what was needed in the fullness of time and seasons.

Gradually, the fires in my heart cooled, and I learned an equal acceptance of what was and would likely never change. Not for them anyway. I was a bit of a different story. Not that I wasn't a good priest. I just wasn't all hellfire and brimstone like some of my colleagues when it came to conversion. Instead, I found myself looking for ways to combine the various beliefs into my own. I suppose you could say they were more successful at converting me than I was them.

So, in my spare time, I became a student of history and all the myriad belief systems of the people that surrounded me. It was a very interesting and enlightening time for me. After many years of wandering the globe, I finally managed to secure a permanent posting. It was exciting and terrifying and exhilarating all at once. I was determined to be the best priest I was capable of.

My first sight of the building was disappointing, to say the least. She stood on a corner, a once grand lady bowed and soured by the passage of time, dark and dour and as unhappy as she could look. The yard was overgrown with weeds. Graffiti marred the brickwork and concrete. Fences and rails were non-existent. The doors were chained shut to prevent looters, and some of the windows were smashed.

But underneath all that, her bones were solid and strong. With a little TLC and a great deal of muscle, she could be great again.

The first thing I did, though, after dropping my few belongings in a room, was climb to the bell tower and pull the rope that dangled there. I'm fairly certain that the resulting *BONG!* destroyed the hearing of a thousand pigeons and scared the daylights out of the neighbourhood. From the amount of dust that filtered down onto me, it had been several years since that had happened. But it lifted my flagging spirits to know that at least that worked. It never occurred to me that dry rot and termites could have made it a dangerous first and last decision on my part.

I won't bore you with the details of hard work and elbow grease, of begging the diocese for funding for repairs and necessary upgrades. Suffice to say that there was a lot of that. A great deal of it my own. But also help from the neighbourhood. Those first years there was a lot of making do, a lot of "We have received your request...." and a lot of bartered labour.

My very first catholic service, I think perhaps ten people showed up. Mostly out of curiosity I suspect than any true need for salvation. But they came and we went through the motions. They were, I think, pleased that the old girl was being cleaned up finally if not filled to capacity, at least used.

But at the end of the service, one gentleman suggested that he knew a guy who might be able to fix up that light. But he wasn't a Catholic.... did that matter? No, as a matter of fact it didn't. When could he come?

The repairman came, dutifully fixed the light, and we chatted. Compared notes and experiences, he being from Bangalore, I having spent time in Delhi. It was a pleasant conversation. The next day, he returned wife and children in tow. Apparently, there was another light that he was concerned about. While he worked, I made tea for the wife and kids, and then let them wander around in the nave for a bit under the watchful eyes of Mother.

"You know. This is a very lovely old building. So much room. And so close to our home," she sighed delicately. "We have to travel all the way across the city to go to the temple with the children. I do not drive. It is hard." Another delicate sigh.

Of course, I knew exactly where this was heading. I think it was the gentlest battering ram I had ever met. "Would you like to come to services here? You would be more than welcome."

"Oh, but you see, we are not Catholic. We would hate to intrude."

"Please feel free to come whenever you wish."

And sure enough, they came. With small household statues of Vishnu and Lakshmi that they quietly addressed as a group. When they left, the little statues stayed behind. So, did another suggestion for someone who might repair the windows? Again, *not catholic*.

So, Buddha was added to our collection of statuary.

It was a young Wicca lady who repaired the aforementioned dry rot in the bell tower.

She brought a scrying bowl and candles.

Yet another gentleman of Taoist belief repaired the wood flooring. He brings flowers and incense frequently.

Our lovely old lady blossomed in her new finery. It seemed that people were always in and out the door, bringing food, lighting candles, saying prayers, celebrating the ups and accepting downs of life.

Eventually, most of the repairs were complete. And, though the stained-glass windows were not quite as monotheistic as most, and the lack of pews certainly raises eyebrows, my congregation and I are pleased with the result.

How the ArchDiocese feels about it, I remain thankfully clueless. My catholic congregation is so small that it figures little in their grander schemes. They never visit. I don't ask for anything anymore, so they have no reason to.

As I sit here, my crinkly, wrinkly, crackly, arthritic old body sponging up the heat of the sun and reminiscing, some things that I never thought about before cross my doddering old mind.

Firstly, I can not really pick a time or a particular moment when my personal ethos made the leap from one God to several. Perhaps it never really did. Perhaps, it was just a matter of accepting that the one possibility is just as valid as the other and should therefore be given equal weight in the consideration of religion. One God and a thousand saints, or several Gods and Goddesses to look after the needs of the world. Is there a difference? Is any one belief right or wrong?

All I know, for certain, is that what works for me, or suits me, may or may not work for you. It depends on your level of comfort and need. It is nearly impossible to totally abandon beliefs that were instilled in a person during the formative years. So, I still celebrate Christmas on its appropriate day. But I also celebrate Yule and Kwanzaa, and Hanukkah with the people of my neighbourhood. Even if they have never set foot in the door. Such is my choice.

Secondly, it amazes me how easily one can encapsulate a life well-lived into a few short sentences. To be sure there are details that are glossed over or not mentioned at all. But all the salient points have been covered, I'm sure. Either way, it took a long time to live it, subjectively. Objectively, it seems like this all happened only yesterday. Funny how that works.

The House of the Enlightened was born.

 A place more about community than any one religion.

A haven for those in need, regardless of *race, creed, or colour*.

Or apparent life....

Most of the pews have been replaced with prayer rugs. The statuary is small, and each belief holds a particular section within the main body of the building. All the wood and brass gleam and sparkle in the light. It all looks marvellous and balanced, warm and inviting. Every Sunday, we hold a service that incorporates all the represented deities. Followed by a luncheon with varied and delightful food choices. The ladies and gents come and go as time allows, each willing to help the other when they can. Children, too, have a place here as an after-school program. I, myself, have been known to join in the games and sing-alongs.

"John Jacob Jingleheimer Schmidt......."

Tale 7: Ramon

Unaccountably nervous, I pick a chair at the back of the semicircle, sit, and try to relax. *It's hard, though.* Most of the people here I have seen before. Usually in less-than-ideal circumstances. Because I'm a cop. They know I'm a cop. So, acceptance of me, of my presence here, is less than certain. If I were a betting man, I'd place my odds at forty to one. *Very long odds.* Maybe I'd be better off going to the meetings run by the department psych's. But there I sensed that my whole life would be hashed over and analyzed; my job performance thoroughly scrutinized, chewed up, spat out, and red flagged for "further study". Yeah sure, according to the union reps, they can't actually do that. But there's a difference between actually can't and actually don't. I trust the 'ologists about as far as I can see them blindfolded. And I'm not too sure of the union reps either.

A youngish guy in slacks and a white button-down walk to the front. *Spontaneously*, I start noticing details and impressions. Hair was short, but not military short.

Clothing is comfortable but not worn out.

Gainfully employed?

No evidence of tats or gang signs.

Glasses, wire-rimmed. Functional, not fancy.

Caucasian. Possibly some Hispanic in there somewhere, though. Or tans easy.

Calm attitude. No tremors or evidence of nervousness.

So, he's used to speaking in front of strangers?

The only offbeat thing?

Adidas, not loafers, well-worn and scuffed with frayed laces.

Runner maybe? Marathoner? Hard to tell under the clothes what physical condition he's in.

"Good evening, everyone. My name is Myles. It's good to see you here tonight. I hope this is as helpful for you as it was for me. You see, I'm an addict. My drug of choice was meth. But I've been drug-free for three years."

Huh. Never would have pegged him for a tweaker.

This may be more interesting (or helpful) than I thought.

"So, who would like to go second since I was the first?" Myles asks.

A few polite snickers, but no one gets up.

My mind is running at *Mach One*.

How much do I tell them?

Do they need to know the whole sordid story?

Will they even care?

Was this a mistake after all?

Geez, where's the bathroom?

Why is it that when you're nervous, the kidneys go into overdrive?

Might as well get it over with. Then I can get outta here before somebody slashes my tires. I stand up, walk slowly to the front, trying to hide what I'm really feeling...cop training. You deal with and save the breakdown for later.

"My name is Ramon. Some of you already know me. Because I'm one of the cops who work in this area." Pause, big breath, "and I'm an alcoholic. It's been seven days since my last drink. And man, it's hard. Especially some days."

"Hi Ramon." the group chants back. A few familiar faces get that hard look. But they don't say anything. Or move.

I continue, "Life is hard. Everywhere. I guess it just shows more in some places. That's why I became a cop in the first place. High ideals: make everyone's life better. However, that looks.

This is the beat they gave me when I first started. Maybe to show me how stupid I was. But I'm still here. But I was definitely green as grass back then. I was so sure that I could change things. Make a difference. It didn't quite work out the way I thought it would." Pause again, and swallow a couple of times because the throat has gotten dry.

Polite laughter and some joker whispered, "*Well no shit, Sherlock.*" which brought more snickers.

On I went some more, "I could see that a lot were trying. But every step they took forward, something, circumstances, life, choices, whatever, pushed them two steps back. I know, as a cop, I'm not supposed to let it bother me. Leave the job in the locker room, don't bring it home."

In my mind's eye, I see a small white nightgown. As always, my eyes burned with tears I couldn't shed. Maybe I should just shut up now. Mouth had other ideas, though.

"But, believe it or not, I'm a human first and a cop second. So, when I see someone alive today and gone the next, it kills me a little inside. I wonder if there was something that I missed or should have done to stop it. So, at night sometimes, I would have a drink to take the edge off. Right? Then one became two, and the rest, as they say, is history."

Felt kind of good to get that out in the open. But my knees were in danger of collapsing now. I started to head back to my seat.

"You're still a cop, though?" Myles asks.

"Yes. I am." I stop and turn to him.

"So, what's different now? The problems will still be there. People, you see, will still die. How are you going to stay sober through all that?"

The only honest answer I can give him is, "One day at a time." And hope that will be enough. After the meeting was over (yeah, I stayed), we gathered around the coffee and snack table. Some of them sure needed the sugary treats and sandwiches more than I did; they were so thin a stiff breeze could have knocked them over. Reminded me of those history pics of concentration camp survivors; too big clothes sagging on emaciated bodies, long-sleeved shirts, and skeletal hands rubbing constantly against the fabric.

For the most part, everyone avoided me, like I had the plague or something. You didn't have to look hard to find the line between *"me"* and *"them"*. Maybe part of that was my fault. Defensive separation, trying to avoid a fight of some kind. Have you ever noticed how some things become so much a part of you that you don't even notice that you're doing it anymore? Like a nervous tic. Or rubbing your hands up and down your arms?

One thing I guess I did get from tonight was not to assume everything is the way it looks...

Myles must have noticed I was pretty much left alone while the rest of them talked. So, he came over. "Good job up there," he says.

Meh.

"Okay. I'm curious. I know there are AA groups aimed specifically at people in the service. So why here? Why this place?"

"Dunno. Seemed right. And I guess maybe if they see me as a man and a cop when I'm working, maybe they'll be, you know, more willing to meet me halfway.

They gotta know that as a cop, I can't let them do something outside the law. If I have to I'll haul them downtown. Or whatever. But maybe they'll know I'm doing it because I have to, not cause I like to. And all I really wanna do is help them get outta the hole that they're in. There are some great people out there. And some not-so-great ones, too. But mostly there's just a whole bunch that are caught in the middle."

"So," Myles smiles side-wise, "The young idealist isn't quite buried under the cop bluster. Be careful, Ramon. It's a fine line you're trying to walk. Don't slip and fall."

***

I watch Ramon Walk out, slightly behind the rest of the group. It would take him a while to assimilate. First, they would have to get over his day job.

So did he, for that matter. I could tell that he was watching all of us with his cop instincts front and center. I saw the flash of surprise when I admitted being an addict myself. Good, it meant he wasn't one hundred percent certain of everything he thought he knew. All in all, I liked the guy.

"Well, John. What do you think?" I ask my unseen mentor.

There wasn't an answer that a *"normal"* person would acknowledge. But in the back of my mind, I distinctly heard a chuckle. I turn off the lights and promptly land on my keister. Somehow my laces are tangled together......

***

What? You think being a GA means I can't have a little fun?

In the Diocese registry, it's known officially as St. Therese of the Roses.

A two-storey brick and stone edifice complete with a functioning bell tower and a stylized rose window over the double oak doors. Built some time in the late 1800s, she has stood on the same corner between two main thoroughfares, virtually unchanged.

Until John Jacob was given the priestship of the grand old lady and her ever-decreasing flock. John always thought that the Church had settled him there because they thought he had "gone native" and needed to be reintegrated into the faith.

Well, they were right.

In getting repairs done to the building, he turned his new home into something more than a simple catholic church. When money wasn't readily available, he bartered space inside the church for labour and materials.

Win-win for St Therese and the neighbourhoods. Since the deacons were getting their needs met (she was, after all, still a functioning church), they turned a blind eye to a few things.

A statue, freshly painted, still stands in the vestibule to greet you, miniature roses growing at her feet in summer, porcelain replicas in winter. There is a cross behind the altar, but the crucified Christ is absent, as are the stations of the cross. The baptismal font is used more often as a scrying bowl. The flowers that are frequently decorated are more of orange and yellow chrysanthemums than lilies. The incense in the censers is more patchouli and sandalwood than frankincense and myrrh, and the stained-glass windows are more eclectic than overtly religious.

The people who use the space bring with them small idols of their faith. Which can occasionally be concealed inside small woven cabinets, should the bishop or some such august personage pay a call.

Mostly, though, silk cloths are used to cover them when not in use.

The idols don't seem to mind over much. Nor apparently, did God...

The House of Enlightenment is a happy functioning community center. Open to any and all that need her. It is not uncommon to see women handing out blankets and food to the half-frozen waifs that come in seeking warmth. Or men for that matter.

John was pleased that it worked out so well.

And then he went and died!!

It was a sad and confusing, and scary time for everyone.

Not only would his final service be officiated by the *Archbishop* and his brother priests, but no one was certain what would become of their center now.

Would the new priest be as kind as John?

Would the Diocese shut it down?

As a testament to John's standing in the community, everyone who could, came to the service. The three pews were quickly filled. So plastic chairs from anywhere and everywhere were pressed into service. Saris and Sherwani suits, Tang jackets, jeans, dark suits, and sombre dresses all melded together before the eyes of the Officials. Turbans, scarves, and ball caps respectfully covered heads. It was a good send-off for a much-loved man.

Afterwards, various groups made certain to finish the process according to their own rites.

So, St. Therese was bustling with people for more than a few days.

Time enough to deal with the other things later....

That couldn't stop me from thinking about it though. There were so many things in the works that could all go sideways if the wrong decision comes down the pipe.

But John keeps assuring me that it will all work out. And as he is closer (especially now) to the *PTB*, I guess I have to believe him.

Tale 8: I/She/We

Melody

So, without realizing it, D and I set up a working relationship of sorts. I was the righter of wrongs, and occasionally, he cleaned up the mess. We let the *PTB* take care of the rest.

It works. No one that doesn't deserve it gets hurt, and the only complaints are from the bad guys, and who listens to them anyway.

I get to hang out wherever I want, unseen, unknown, and D gets to do his thing.

Sometimes on slow nights (not that there is such a thing as slow in the city), we hang out together, just watching as the neighbourhood goes through the motions. Once in a while, I traipse along behind D and observe from the shadows.

Funny. I never realized there was an art to his job. A certain delicacy. He says it has to do with timing. Personally, I think he's just a big old softie.

I wish I could be. But in my own line of work, soft wouldn't get much done. Being nice to the jerks I deal with regularly wouldn't change a damn thing. By the time I show up, they've all reached the point where nice is the same as weak (or so THEY think).

Sure, at one point, they were all little kids, and maybe they became jerks because of some other ass-hole who took the nice right out of them. Maybe, given the right circumstances, they might have changed for the better. *Maybe*. But at some point, they chose to become and stay the mean, angry person they are.

 There's nothing that can be done about yesterday except to learn from it. But that won't change the consequences any. Dues still have to be paid.

Yeah. I know. I don't sound like I'm much better than the thugs I hunt.

But I came into being because one of those jerks tried to kill my mom and ended up getting me -and himself- killed instead. And I could have gone on.

But I didn't.

I stayed. I made myself grow up. I gave myself a costume. I became THIS! The embodiment of anger. Because at the time of my passing, I was angry, and so were the people I cared about.

Anger is an emotion that I understand, and there is a lot of stuff that makes people angry. Sometimes it's stuff that I can do something about.

The problem is, the more I hang out with D, the more I wonder if there isn't more to this whole living thing besides anger. Sometimes after a long shift, I follow him to a part of town that isn't his regular beat. He stops at this big old brick building but never goes inside. He just stands there and looks. Kinda weird. But it seems to make him feel better.

Some day, maybe I'll ask him about it. Probably not, though. Even D is allowed some privacy, *I think*.

Once in a while, I follow one of the other "incarnations" that are out there. But there's just something about mine that is more interesting. Or maybe more human?

I have no idea how long he's been D, or who he was before. Just another one of those things we don't talk about.

Time runs kinda funny for us anyway. I have no idea how long I've been me either. I watch the seasons come and go in a very limited way. For the most part they don't affect me. I see it. I hear it. But it doesn't touch me with heat or cold or whatever.

I remember what they used to feel like, though.

The one season that I find particularly challenging is *"Christmas"*.

I see the pretty lights and Santas everywhere, the snowflakes falling, bright white in the street lights, the bells, the glitz, the people with arms full of packages, Yada!! Yada!!. And it makes my heart (if I still had one) hurt.

So, I spend the majority of that time holed up in the deepest, darkest, most forgotten corner of the library. I read. I think. I try not to remember anything that has anything to do with Christmas.

Yes. I become Scrooge for a time.

What of it???

How sad is a life when the dark times of it stretch behind you like a parade of sad clown faces and broken glass, but the happy times can be counted on the fingers of your hands? How bad is it when the pain and hunger and sadness seem more normal than the touch of a clean, soft blanket, a gentle smile, or the sloppy kisses of a puppy, which are more the stuff of dreams than reality?

This is the place I came from. My own name has been forgotten. Gibbering terror and cold to mark the passing of time. *Anxiety, hunger,* and *Death* were my only companions. Never looking up or beyond because all I had was "*Now*".

There were faceless kindnesses given to the hundreds like me: a bag of not quite rotten food left to be found by whichever of us got there first; a bottle of water occasionally here or there; the garbage men who ignored the pile of boxes and rags in the corner by the dumpster because they knew it was someone's home; the young grocery clerks carefully setting out some edibles knowing there was a gang of us hiding behind the crates, waiting.

There were also, of course, the "*soup kitchens*" where you could get a hot meal once in a while if you were willing and desperate enough to subject yourself to the harangue of "your sins and base nature that brought you to this lowly state was the mark of the Devil upon you. Repent and all shall be made new!"

I never found it particularly uplifting to be brow-beaten while I tried to eat. But there were a few that did. And good for them. I hope they found the peace they sought in the end.

No. It was chance, pure and simple, that led me to the House of the Enlightened that day. Well, chance and Rennie.

It was their unasked-for help and simple caring that, slowly, brought me back from the feral, almost human, to a person. With a name and everything!

A long journey that began with a warm bowl of soup and a sandwich.

I could talk about the long days of change that happened so slowly but were occasionally too fast. I could talk about hot meals that came sermon free. Of a warm place to sleep and warm blankets. I could talk about the bliss of having an all over bath, scrubbing off layers of grime and skin until you felt clean. Of someone patiently brushing and detangling your hair. I could tell you about the feel of new-to-me clean clothes gently rubbing pink, sensitive skin.

The best part, though, is the people who run the House of Enlightenment.

Men and women. Christians of no particular *faith, Muslims, Buddhists, Wicca-Pagan, Agnostics,* and *Atheists*. A whole group of people with different beliefs who see a need, in themselves, and the world around them, and decide to do what they can to help. Not for profit. Not for glory. Not for any reason other than they are willing. No fighting. No debates. Just respect for each other's differences and talents.

It is a magical place.

And I am more than grateful for everything that they've done for me. My name is Chelsea Schmidt now. I have a job and my own little apartment, not too far from the House. I should be ecstatic. I should be over the moon with happiness. And mostly I am.

Especially during holidays. But especially Christmas.

The two of us lived in a dingy little apartment in a run-down apartment building. The plaster walls cracked and graffiti covered; the rugs in the hallways were stained with every imaginable substance; the place reeked of mould and other things; garbage was strewn randomly; stray cats and dogs (and probably rats) roamed freely in the halls because the outside doors never closed properly. Nobody who lived there had anything nice. Because if they did, it was gone two seconds later. Cops were regular visitors to one neighbour or another.

Welfare checks every month kept the lights on and put a little food in the barely working refrigerator, and sometimes clothes showed up that were obviously used but better than what we had.

She would get a job. Work for a little while, stay clean and out of trouble. Give up the night life. An idyll that could never last.

Sure, for a while it worked. But then the yelling would start and the slaps and the tears and the shakes. So, she would disappear for a night, often leaving me alone because finding a babysitter was impossibly hard. In the morning, she would come back, smudged and musky-smelling and more often than not, high as a kite. There would be a few extra dollars in her bag, so she would take me for pizza or something.

For that little time life would be great. But ups were always followed by downs. I actually got pretty good at predicting when they would happen so I could make myself as non-intrusive as possible for as long as possible.

Holidays were the worst. She wanted to get the nice things. She wanted to make it special. But every spare dollar went up her nose or in her arm or whatever was good at the moment.

But Christmas was always the worst.

Mom tried, in her way, to make it nice. She would come home one day with a branch or two off a pine, the end cracked and twisted where she broke it off the tree. She would tie a big ribbon around it and hang it on the wall. For a while, the dingy apartment smelled nice. Then there would be the small present wrapped and waiting for Christmas morning underneath it. Until she "needed" and then that little something would disappear. Most likely back to the pawn shop where she got it in the first place. Naturally, she felt remorse and sadness and made all sorts of promises that she would never be able to keep. I would hug her and forgive her. And she would sometimes, in her delirium, call me by another name. Then I would help her down the street to the soup kitchen, and we would eat whatever they had. Sometimes it was turkey. Most times not.

And then the boughs would dry up and die, and she'd be screaming about the mess.

And that was *Christmas*.

At one point, some do-gooder called Children's Services on us. But somehow, we managed to slip past all that. Until the day that Mom took a hot shot and disappeared. There was no evading CS then. Foster care, here I come.

And about the only thing I can think of that was good about that whole shit show, was that I had clean clothes and went to school. Evading the boys and "Father's" advances was a full-time job. Until one day, I lost.

But of course, it was my fault. I led him on. He's a good man. Really. He would never! She's an incorrigible little liar. No better than her Mother!! Blood tells you know!! Blah Blah Blah.

I ran. Back to the neighbourhood, I understood. To the people who knew me.

Of course they were all gone, or didn't want to know me. So "*Kip*" was born. Of nothing. With nothing. From nothing. And likely to become nothing.

So here I am now, in this building full of light and laughter and colour and delicious food smells. Doing my best to be a part of it all. To act like I fit in here. To forget everything that was and think of everything that is and could be mine.

But inside?

Where no one can see?

A little girl wrapped in a grey cloud that makes her hazy and indistinct but no less real, lies curled up in a small pool of cold light. She sobs quietly there alone. Her sorrow steals what happiness lies around me. Her coldness steals my warmth.

I wish I could die.

So here I am, curled up in a window seat (OK I cheated. It's just a ledge in front of a grimy window, but I "found" some pillows and made it comfy), reading a thick dusty old volume of War and Peace. Which was actually kinda neat because each line was written in Russian with the English words' underneath. I think I was reading it more so I could study the Russian characters than for the actual story.

I haven't been outside for days. I'm safely ensconced here. No reason to leave. No desire to either. Hibernating, ghosty style.

"Hey!! squirt," says D as he walks around the desks, tables, and book-piled chairs.

"Hey!! yourself, Big Guy. You lost or something?" highly unlikely, but I know for certain that there isn't a living person anywhere inside this building.

"Nope. Not lost. Too early for my shift to start. Haven't seen you around a lot lately."

"And you were all worried about me? That's nice. But totally unnecessary." I lift the mega volume and hide my face behind it. Hoping he'd go away.

But one of his hands (I never realized how big they are!) pushes the book down and he looks at me all serious and stuff, "Melody. I have someplace I want to go. I was wondering if you would come with me." he adds a bit of a smile, "Please."

"Yah? Where?" intrigued in spite of myself. He's never outright invited me along before.

"Someplace sort of special to me."

Now what place, short of his own grave, would be special to Death?

Well of course I went. Don't be an idiot.

I suppose I really shouldn't be surprised. A couple of blocks and a few turns later, D and I are standing in front of the brick building that he likes to visit for no apparent reason.

Like everything at this time of the year it had the usual decorations on the doors; wreaths and battery-operated candles. I could hear the sound of music and voices faintly. So, there was some celebration of some sort going on. *Meh.*

D stopped on the sidewalk. He watched me for a bit, a strange look in his eyes.

"Ok. So, we're here." I was more than a little grumpy about it now. I thought we were going on some grand adventure. Instead, we are standing in front of some nameless rock pile in the cold and snow. "What's the big deal?"

"Do you know what this place is? You've followed me here often enough," he asked calmly.

"Nope. And if that's what you wanna show me, you've shown me. I've seen it. Leaving now." I answer belligerently.

"You really don't see him, do you?" softly, wonderingly, and confused.

"See who? Nobody here but us and a few humans." What was he talking about? Could Death get senile? "You're losing it, Big Guy."

"No. I'm not. Come here for a minute." he reaches out one of his big hands. In the light I can see the callouses that will never fade, the white circle where a ring once lay and faded scars. A working man's hands.

I hesitated, then let that big old mitt wrap around my own hand.

And we were inside the building.

And there was an old guy, dressed in the black smock and pants of the clergy, smiling a crinkly, warm smile at me.

AT ME!!! Wait! What????

"Hello, Melody. "I've been waiting to meet you," he says. His eyes are the brightest blue I have ever seen, full of warmth. There are laugh lines around them. He laughed softly while I just stood there, gawping. "You can call me John."

Stunned, I automatically shake the hand he offers. "But how? I mean, who? You know my name..." I manage to stammer. Oh, go me! Articulate and succinct. NOT!

"Yes, I know your name. Actually, I know a great deal about you and how special you are. Not to mention how special you could be."

 And then he tilts his snowy head towards the inside where all the people are, "But there are a couple of people I'd like you to meet before I explain. Come with me? Please?"

I must have still been in a daze, because I let him lead me into the (and I could tell now) church. He stopped behind a middle-aged man who was clapping his hands as the music played.

"Do you know who this is?" John asks. I shake my head no. "This is Ramon. He has a deep sadness in him. Can you tell what it is?"

I look at him. I "listen" a little. Revenge was nowhere to be found. But I did see a face. Young. Female. About eight years old. Darkish blonde hair. Skinny. Someone is putting her in a car while he watches, all sad and needing a drink because he was sad. Poor guy.

"Something about a girl," I say.

"Good. Now look over there. He doesn't see it yet because he is new here. But look closely at that girl over there by the door."

It takes me a moment to see it, but sure enough, there it is as plain as paper. That young woman over there is the same little girl that he was sad about. "Wow!" I whisper.

"Very good. Now, look a little deeper at Ramon. Because she isn't the only thing that makes him sad."

So, I look. Deeper. He's younger now. In a car with his partner. A call and they are racing to some run-down old building. A guy comes lumbering out of the alley with a little kid in a bloody nightgown over his shoulder........

My eyes must have gotten as big as dinner plates. "Is that the guy who shot Floyd?"

"Well, he thinks he is," John answers. "If you could say anything to Ramon about that night, and he could hear you, what would it be, do you think?"

I hate being put on the spot like that! Sensible words don't just roll off my tongue at the drop of a hat. But I couldn't not answer John either. "I suppose I would tell him it was okay. I mean, if he was the one who shot Floyd, Floyd deserved it. Either way, I was gonna die that night... Right D? So, it wasn't really his fault. He was never the one that I was angry at. You either D." I managed to say. And then looked down at my toes, embarrassed.

"Ok. Let's go visit the young lady."

"Why?" I let curiosity out to play.

"Well, Ramon needs to know she's okay. And there might be a thing or two that needs knowing there too," he answered. Smugly, I thought.

So, we weave our way through the crowd. I noticed that John, like D, tried to avoid touching them. Weird. The girl is standing at the back of the group, singing and clapping like the rest, but even I could tell she wasn't overly excited by the whole thing. I tended to agree.

"As before. Take a look. See what can be seen." John says softly.

This one was surprisingly easy. She was wide open. Nothing held in. But everything was grey and fuzzy like I was looking through an old gauze cloth: the time on the streets, living in boxes, sleeping in garbage, eating out of dumpsters. Being cold and scared.

Poor kid! It occurred to me that it might have been me if things had been different...

Look deeper. A face. Thin and hollow-cheeked, eyes feverish, the briefest glimpse of a torso with puckered marks where (a knife??) had been forced through the skin....

 I pulled back a little. NO WAY!!!

A little more ruthless now, I dive back in, focus on that woman.

"I'm so sorry baby," she says through hiccuppy sobs. "Mommy is so sorry." the woman cries.

"It's okay, Mama. I love you," little Aria says, holding the woman with her skinny little arms.

"Oh, Mommy loves you too, Melody," she says as she passes out.

And Oh, my gawd! I stumbled back and would have fallen if D hadn't been standing right there. John looked on, smiling like the cat that had just licked up all the cream

Holy Shit!!! I have a sister!!!

It was a lot to process. Without even thinking about it I blinked out. Went to the roof of my apartment building to storm and stomp and.... process.

D gave me until the next day before he came to find me again. I was still angry. Toweringly so. But I was also awestruck! I wasn't alone in the world anymore. Aria wasn't alone in the world anymore. I mean, we couldn't really be besties or anything like that. But I am a big sis. Which means I'm supposed to look after my little sis, right?

But how the heck was I gonna do that when I am on a whole different plane of existence than her? GAH!!!!

"You knew!" I yelled as soon as I saw him. "You FUCKING knew and didn't say anything!" I stomped around a few times.

"No. We suspected. But we couldn't go deep enough. I for sure can't read people's hearts, and John was afraid that his own perceptions of things would skew it. So, we needed you to look." he said, using that reasonable, infuriating, adult voice that makes me nuts.

"Well, now what genius? She's there and I'm here and there's a whole world of difference between us now." I almost started bawling, which I hate to admit.

"Talk to John. He might have an idea or two. Gotta go. Duty calls." and he blinked away, leaving me almost as confused as I was before he got there.

Seeing no other option, I went to see John. He was waiting for me on the steps of the church.

Huh.

Not being disposed to kindness just yet, I blurted out, "Now what?"

"Now we start by making sure that the two of them meet. Her name is Chelsea now by the way. Aria was a lifetime ago."

So, I followed John into the House of Enlightenment, and we set to work.

I gotta say it was kinda strange having a partner besides D. It was even stranger to be working on something that, we hoped, would make a few people happy.

As it turned out, Ramon had just joined the AA meetings that were taking place in the basement of the House. So, getting him there wasn't as big a deal as I thought. Aria/Chelsea proved to be more of a challenge.

Like all little sisters, she wanted to have nothing to do with me or what I wanted her to do, and if I pushed too hard, I was afraid I'd fry her brain.

In the end, it was serendipity (whoever the heck she is) that did the job for us.

Ramon was at his meeting. He volunteered to come up to the kitchen to get more sugar or something. And who should be working in the kitchen that night? My little sis (You know I still get this little chill thing down my back when I think about that).

Anyway....

They start to talk...and talk....and talk....

John and I just stood back and watched. Even from there I could see the grey haze lifting a little from around Chelsea and Ramon didn't seem so desperately sad. It was nice. Nobody likes to think they are all alone in the world. So, a connection of any kind is better than none at all.

"So. Now that we have that out of the way, would you like to know what's next?" John asks.

"Back to business as usual, I guess. But I'll keep an eye on these two when I can." I answer.

"Would you like to do more things like this? Trying to make sure that a few people are safe and happy more often?"

"Can't say I've really thought about it much. Does feels kinda nice, though." I admit.

"Do you suppose instead of thinking of yourself as a being of revenge, you might redefine yourself as a sort of Guardian Angel?"

"Depends. Do I have to have wings and talk to the Big Guys all the time?" I dislike authority figures.

"I shouldn't think so. It's just that you'll be changing your focus a little bit. That word isn't going to bother you as much, or at least not in the same way, that it used to."

"Hmmmm."

The End.

Oh, I do hope Melody enjoys her raise.

Not that revenge isn't necessary occasionally.

But helping people deliberately is infinitely more satisfying.

And I'm sure John will keep an eye on her.

Tale 9: G.A.I.T

Guardian Angel in Training

Wow! I have a sister! Still blows me away when I think about it! One minute I'm *Melody/Revenge*, all alone in the world, doing my thing. Next, I'm a big sister and a GAIT (Guardian Angel in Training). Like, how cool is that!! Of course, there's a downside, too.

Being an adult now kinda sucks. There are rules, apparently. A lot of rules. I miss the carefree days of being able to do what I wanted with nobody looking over my shoulder. Well, except maybe D once in a while. But he never stopped me from doing stuff. He just made me think about it sometimes. Now, I traipse along beside John and listen while he explains things. He's a good teacher. Nice guy too. But he asks these questions that I have no idea how to answer.

Gives me a headache.

Is a bad thing done for the right reason the same as a good thing done for a good reason?

And what about good things done for bad reasons?

What came first? The chicken or the egg?

In my spare time, my before existence, I spent some time reading in the library. Not little kids' books either. I thought I was pretty smart. All those books on theory and psychology and like that. But I guess reading it isn't the same as understanding it. And you can't really understand it until you try it or apply it. And trying and applying and understanding, isn't the same as believing and knowing what actually works.

He says I'll figure some of it out eventually.

I need an aspirin....

So today, John and I are going to visit a few people that he's been keeping an eye on for a while. He says now that he's not "tied to a physical body," it's a lot easier. He just thinks about them, and poof, there he is.

In order for me to tag along, I have to be holding his hand. Something to do with me not knowing these people like he does, and being a trainee. It's a little confusing. Before, the only thing I needed to find someone was for them to be thinking of the word *"revenge"* strongly enough that it got my attention. But that word doesn't affect me anymore. So, it's identities, not words that draw me....

See... rules.

I wonder if there's a handbook that I should be reading to explain all this...stuff.

First up: Petey and Gina.

An eye blink later, John and I are standing in an abandoned shack at the back of an old warehouse complex. The place smells of old oil and grease. So, it's safe to assume that it used to be a tool shed of some kind. You know that *garagey* kind of smell that never leaves even after the tools and equipment are gone. It isn't much of a place. The one window is boarded up, so it's dingy and dark. But they've gone to the trouble to make it, *homey.* A fireplace made out of cement blocks and a tin flue is in one corner away from the door (which is the only exit), and is wisely vented outside so they can breathe. But I wouldn't want to insure it against fire. A stack of old blankets is neatly piled nearby. A small board with pop bottle legs is in the middle, and it's old and stained, but a rug is laid out to cover the dirt floor.

Gina is sitting on the rug close to the fireplace. Not doing much.

But rubbing her bulging stomach.....

Oh, good grief!! Is that what I think it is?

"John! Seriously? We have to do something! There's no way that she can... not here!"

"I know. And I've been trying to think of a way to get them to a better place. But they are stubborn. And untrusting," he sighs a great sigh.

"Something will have to happen soon, though..."

Well duh! She looks like she could pop any minute. I start thinking about all the people I know who might be able to help.

Chelsea? Nope. Dragging her back here might upset the apple cart.

Ramon? Again nope. These kids don't trust cops.

Then who? Who do I know that is minimally threatening that can help these kids?

Another rule: we work through others if we can't get the attention of our- clients. Rarely do we work directly. John calls its networking.

"So, where's Petey?" It just occurred that he is MIA.

A blink later and we find him. Scavenging in the neighbourhood dumpsters for food. He has an old grocery cart with him that has some other stuff, more blankets, wooden things, and what not. My heart broke for the poor guy. I did see that he was being particularly choosy about the food, though. I assumed he was saving that for Gina. Sure, hoped so anyway. But, I/We definitely had to get this situation sorted, and fast.

"Is there anybody at the House that can do anything?" I asked quietly.

"We have that little area in the back. You know the one we set up for Chelsea? But nobody has been able to convince them to come. They show up for food sometimes, but that's as close as they get." John sighs another great, sad sigh.

"Could Chelsea talk to them, maybe?" I wondered out loud. "I hate to get her involved, now that we have her in a good place. But she might be the only one who can convince these kids it's their best option for now."

"That might work. I wonder why I didn't think of that. Must be getting old."

I looked sidewise at him, finally catching on. Wisely, I said nothing. So, because Chelsea was at work right then, contacting her would have to wait. Which meant Petey and Gina would have to wait as well. I hoped that Gina would give us enough time. Next up was Georgianna. Her, I knew from sitting in on the AA meetings that Myles was conducting at the House.

Rail thin. Borderline skeletal. Only recently off the stuff, and having a hard time dealing with it. Trying really hard though. The situation wasn't easy because her pusher/pimp wouldn't leave her alone. It seemed he wanted her back.

We blinked in as Georgi was slinking (I know, but how else can I say it, she was walking from doorway to doorway, always looking around before she moved, avoiding eye contact or contact in general, being furtive) down a side street. Obviously, she was headed somewhere. I got the impression it wasn't a good place. She was carrying something in a paper bag, holding it close to her scrawny chest like her life depended on it. I wasn't sure I wanted to know what was in that bag. But when I looked up the street, I could see Roy- the aforementioned dickhead- leaning against a building.

I looked at John. John looked at me.

"Where's Ramon?

Right now?" I snapped.

Ok. So, a little bit of the old me was still there.

I blinked out.

As luck would have it, Ramon was on shift. Alone. Half a block away. Having never done this totally on my own before, I touched him on the shoulder and "thought" about Georgi and Roy and where they were and what was likely going to happen.

"*Please, Please, Please*! Hear me, Ramon. Get there as fast and as quietly as you can." I whispered in his ear. "You gotta catch this scumbag. Before Georgi does something, she'll regret."

Amazingly, it worked. He turned down a different street and came up the back alley behind the building where Roy was waiting for Georgi. I blinked back to John. Who was waiting patiently where I had left him. Problem though. He wasn't alone. One of the other D's was there too.

"Oh no, no no. Please tell me this wasn't a surprise addition to your list!" I said.

Unlike my D, this one just looked at me with cold, dead eyes. And said nothing.

All John or I could do was stand there and watch as it played out. I had my fingers crossed behind my back, hoping it wasn't Georgi or Ramon on that list. If I could have, I would have started bawling right then and there. It seemed that the PTB was listening. Or maybe it had been intended to play out this way. I don't know. But at the end of it all, which by the way seemed to take forever but was only a few minutes, Roy was the one bleeding in the street and Ramon was holding Georgi making sure she was okay. I let out a big breath. And did not watch as this D did his thing. I saw John wince, though.

Sure, that I was going to get into trouble for acting precipitously, I hung my head and waited for him to start lecturing me. He didn't. He just took my hand and we blinked in on Rosemary. A cute little apartment is where we ended up. The walls were in need of some repair and a good coat of paint, the furniture was old and shabby, but colourful pillows and blankets covered the worst of the wear. The kitchen was serviceable and scrupulously clean, baby bottles upended in the rack, drying. A small basket of soft toys sat in a corner, ready for their owner.

I thought to myself, "Oh good. A regular person." Whatever the heck regular actually is????

I shoulda known better.

We could hear a woman's voice crooning softly in the bedroom, so we walked through the little apartment (took about five seconds) and entered the bedroom. The bed was neatly made. The tiny dresser had small woman things arranged neatly on top. In the corner was an empty, white painted crib with baby blankets and little pillows and a mobile clipped to the headboard. There was also a white rocker positioned so you had to go around it to see the woman and the baby when you came in. It wasn't really necessary, but I tiptoed around the chair, already relaxed and smiling, sure that I would see a young woman rocking her baby to sleep.

What I expected and what was, stopped at a woman rocking.

Yup. It was a woman, right enough. But she had left "young" behind long ago. Her hair was long and tangled and pretty much matched the rest of her, which was a mess. Like, Georgi, she was skeletal and wasted. But her faded house dress was clean. She was crooning a lullaby to a bundle in her arms.

"Oh please, do not let that be what's left of a real baby!" I prayed. But I couldn't stop myself from looking.

OH, Thank the *PTB*! It was just a doll!!

I looked at John. He shook his head. There was nothing we could do.

Gently, I touched her shoulder, actual tears pricking at my eyes.

In her mind, Rosemary was sitting in the sunshine, young and beautiful. She was rocking her new born daughter and crooning the same lullaby. The baby was gazing up at her mother with bright adoring eyes, little bubbles coming out of her tiny lips.

It was peaceful and happy there.

"How long?" I had to ask.

"Soon, I think," John replies.

"Good. I hope she's on My D's list. Not that ass from this morning." I patted the bony shoulder, "I'll be back." I said. "Would you mind staying here with her until then? Please. I don't want her to be alone when D gets here."

I blinked myself to Chelsea hoping this wasn't going to be a hard sell. After seeing Rosemary, I needed to do this for Petey and Gina and their baby more than anything in the whole world. It was like a physical pain that I couldn't get rid of. Because there was no aspirin or Tylenol that would get rid of it. She was sitting on her little sofa, reading. *Huh*. Musta have been a good day today. On bad days, she cleans like a crazy thing, needing the physical release to help deal with whatever it was. Some people *eat*. Some people *drink*. My sister *cleans*. For hours. I know, I've watched her.

"Sis? Can you hear me?" I say. No physical reaction, but she didn't turn the page either (I think she speed reads).

"I need you to do me a huge solid."

I move around and park my butt on the coffee table in front of her, paying no attention whatsoever to the things that are sitting there already. I mean, why would I? No physical body. But if she could see me, I imagine it looked pretty corny having a plant sticking outta my middle that way and a steaming cup of tea where my left knee is. She marked her place in the book and laid it aside. Then casually moved the plant to the other side of the table and picked up her tea.

Do you remember seeing Petey and Gina around the House?" I pictured the two of them. Chelsea sipped her tea.

"You know Gina is preggers, right? Well, she's about ready to pop, and the place where they live is not a good place to be having a baby." I pictured the little tool shed.

Chelsea sipped her tea and looked over the rim of her cup.

"I need you to go there and convince them to come to your old place behind the House. It's at least clean and warm there. And the ladies can help her if anything happens. Could you do that do you think? Remember how you felt when you and Rennie first got there? Well, they don't trust anybody either. But I'm afraid something bad will happen if we don't at least get them to the House. Pretty, pretty, please? I'll be there with you. I won't let anything bad happen to you. I promise."

Chelsea finished her tea and took the cup to the sink. Then she whistled for Rennie, who let out a happy little bark, and we went out into the semi-dark. It didn't take very long for the three of us to get to the old warehouse. It was closer than I thought. We did have to walk by a couple of bars, though, so we crossed the street and kept to the shadows. I don't know how it felt for her, but for me it was like old home week. Chelsea looked around carefully before she went through the hole in the fence and walked to the back of the yard. Every few steps, she stopped to listen. When she was satisfied, she carried on. Rennie, bless his yappy little heart, was as quiet as a mouse the whole time.

At the door to the shed, Chelsea knocked and waited politely until someone- Petey, as it turned out- answered the door. Which means he opened it an inch and a half and said, "*Yeah?*"

"Hi. I'm Chelsea. Do you remember seeing me at H.O.E.? Can I come in a minute?"

For the second time that day, the PTB must have been on my side. Even as suspicious as he was, Petey opened the door just wide enough for Chels and Rennie to slip through. I decided to stay outside and play guard while the three of them had their chat. I kept my feelers out, though, so I could sense how this was playing out. If need be, I was willing to go inside and add a little torque to the pleading. It took a while. I think my sis ended up telling some of her own story to the kids to help convince them that it was a worthwhile idea. And that no one there would force them to go anywhere or do anything that they didn't want. I'm equally sure that that dumb, mangy little mutt may have added his two cents' worth of conniving to the whole affair as well. Nubby little tail wagging, tongue lolling out, liquid eyes.. You get the idea.

Whatever and however, it worked.

Petey gathered the few things that they couldn't leave behind (including a wooden rattle that he was carving himself) and threw it into the grocery cart. Slowly and carefully, we got Gina up and waddling through the fence and down the street. It was slow going. I'm sure everyone was grateful that it wasn't a long hike. By the end, Gina was sweating heavily, and Petey got more worried by the minute.

But we made it.

The little tent and the two beds were all set up and warm. There was a pot of soup and a tray of sandwiches waiting. There were clean towels and some water to wash with as well. Myles (it had to have been him because he's the only one we can talk directly to if we need to) had thought of everything. Chelsea and Rennie helped get them all settled. I went back to Rosemary's. To wait. Minutes, or was it hours later? My D showed up.

"Hey Big Guy. Long time no see." I said, smiling even though there were tears running down my face.

"Hey, kid. How is it in the Big Leagues?" he replies.

"Today sucked. But it'll suck a little less soon."

"Yeah." he says, then gentle as you please, he takes Rosemary's young hand, and she and her tiny daughter walk away with him.

To whatever came next.

I stood there and watched them go. Nobody turned to acknowledge that I was there, and that didn't matter. That isn't what I'm here for. John came and gathered me up and took me home to the House. He didn't say anything. But I'm pretty sure there were happy tears in his eyes, too as he blinked us away.

Adult rule: Even as Guardians, we have to consider every decision that we make within the larger picture.

Sometimes those actions may have unintended results. There are things that we can do something about. But there are also things we cannot, or should not, do anything about. The trick is to know the difference.

Now, where the heck did I put that aspirin???

Tale 10: Karun Gupta

It is one of those rare moments at the House when there aren't a lot of people bustling about, so I decide to take advantage of the relative quiet and meditate a little. Or try to. Meditation really isn't my strong suit; too busy a mind, I think, to find the calm centre needed to get into it. But I will try anyway. Truthfully, it's slightly easier here than at my apartment. Something about the House of Enlightenment blocks a lot of the voices that frequently disturb my peace. At home, they are a cacophony of people and spirits with needs and desires and wants and sorrows. Too many and too much to deal with all at once. But naturally they ALL want my undivided attention at the same damn time.

Here, at least, they are reduced to a low hum, like white noise, and I can pick and choose who to deal with, or not deal with any of them at all, if I want. It's a rather novel experience. It seems that most of my life, they've been there, picking at me, demanding attention. When I was a little kid, I would tell my parents about this lady or that man, and they would just brush it off as childish imagination.

"Go play with your imaginary friends, Myles darling. Mommy and Daddy have a lot of work to do."

They would go back to their paperwork on committee meetings and board meetings and ignore me until bedtime. When the current Nanny had me all jammied and clean, they would come up to my room and give me a dutiful kiss good night, wish me sweet dreams, and be gone. Again. When I was older, probably a tween, the voices got more demanding, more aggressive. It wasn't uncommon to lose myself for a time, only to come back inside, not knowing how I got there or what I was doing. It disturbed the housekeeper enough that she had a chat with my parents...

That led me to doctors. Then, therapists and a trial run of some fairly exhaustive (for me anyway) psychotropic pills. Some made it a little better. Most did nothing at all or made it even worse. I often woke up screaming and sweating from "*nightmares*". I wished that someone would drop me down an oubliette and let me go crazy alone. Then a buddy got me high for the first time, and even though the voices were still there, I just didn't care anymore. Not my circus, not my monkeys. It was a relief to be free. So, I did it *again*. And *again*. And *again*.

Not that good old mom and dad, loving parents that they were, noticed. Until other stuff started to happen. Or not happen as the case may be. And this was so not meditating. More like a barefoot walk down a memory lane full of broken bottles and other pokey things! *Disgusted with myself*, I got up and stretched the kinks out. I turned to go to the kitchen when I noticed Karun Gupta kneeling by the little altar of *Vishnu*, whispering prayers.

Ordinarily, I notice when people are using the altars, but I don't "*pay attention*" to it as it is a deeply personal act that really isn't any of my business. This time, the waves of misery and fear were coming off the man in waves so thick I could have chewed them. And if that wasn't enough to ensure I step in, the fact that the jet-black eye of the little statue winking at me certainly was!

Subtle. Very subtle.

I waited patiently while he completed his prayers and offerings, trying to get a mental picture from the "waves" to better understand the problem and how to approach it. It didn't do me any good. My talent for empathetic understanding is limited at best.

"Hey Karun," I say softly, as he takes his final bow. "Is everything okay?"

"I certainly hope so, Mr. Myles," he says as he heads for the door.

Ok so obviously he either doesn't trust me enough to tell me or it's a really personal matter that he won't discuss. Now what do I do?

"I was just going to the kitchen for a cup of tea. Join me?" I offer. Karun hesitates.

I can almost see the wheels turning in his head. Politely refuse? Quietly accept.

"When one asks one's God for assistance, one should look for that assistance wherever he may," came out of my mouth next, much to my surprise, because that wasn't what I was thinking.

Okay.... Since there didn't appear to be anything I could personally add, I headed to the kitchen. He would follow or he would not. *His choice now*. I filled the kettle with water and plugged it in, got out two cups (even though he hadn't come in yet), selected tea bags at random, and waited. It didn't take long. He sat on the island stool and contemplated his clasped hands while I made the tea for the two of us. *Earl Grey*, his favourite, as it turned out. Funny how that works....

"Forgive me, Mr. Myles. I did not mean to offend you when you asked me...."

"You did not offend me. I could see you were upset. I only want to help." I replied mildly.

Do I tell the poor guy that Lord Vishnu borrowed my tongue for a moment?

A new experience that I would have to consider later.

"Want to talk about it? A burden shared lightens the weight on the heart."

"That is very kind of you, Mr. Myles. But I do not see how you can help me."

"Well, let's start with the problem, whatever it is. Then we shall see."

Karun sipped his tea and gathered his thoughts, "It is my son, you see. A good boy. Or at least he used to be. But of late, he has been hanging around with a bad crowd of boys. I am afraid for him."

"Bad crowd of boys? What are these boys doing when you see them? How old are they? About the same age as your son?"

"Junaid is only fourteen. The boys who are his new friends are perhaps a little older. When I see them, they are usually on street corners, not doing much except talking and laughing. It is the clothes that makes me worry. It is most likely just a fatherly concern for his only son. My sweet Aruna says not to worry so much. It is just a phase that he will outgrow. Soon we will have to consider his future and his wife. I want him to marry well. If there are darknesses in his history, it will be more difficult to find the perfect bride. And, then there is the little shop to consider as well. Junaid will take it over one day. As I got it from my father. I should not have bothered you with my little problems."

"And yet you are concerned enough that you would seek guidance from Vishnu. It seems to me that it bothers you a great deal. And if it bothers you that much, then it is not a "little" problem at all."

I'm not really a touchy feely kinda guy but I reached out and took Karun's brown hand in mine for a moment and gave it a gentle (but manly) squeeze.

"Let me look into it a little. Perhaps there is something I can do. Or perhaps someone else who can help."

Get Ramon to pull up a rap sheet on them maybe. But first, I would need names and descriptions. Which meant taking a walk. It took a few days before I found the time. Okay, that's a lie. It took me a few days to screw up the courage to go. I knew where KG Indian market was located a few blocks away from H.O.E. Too short a distance to bother driving. The problem was that the few blocks also contained my old haunts from the weeks and months that I spent high. Places that I scrupulously avoided since giving up that life (*Thank you again, John*!).

Now I would have to walk by them.

Which likely meant I would remember how it felt. See people that I wanted to forget.

Would I have the strength to resist? I knew it was bound to happen sometime.

 I had hoped that it would be a hundred years later than this, though.

Frankly, I was scared spitless. And I hated myself for it. Before I started out, I asked John and Melody to be with me as I made the journey. There was no answering echo in my head to let me know they had heard.

All journeys begin with a single step....

It was hard, walking by, smelling the familiar things, some sweet, some sour. It made my nose twitch, and because scent is the strongest memory inducer known to man, I remembered. *The good times. The bad times. The faces.*

The most difficult was when I walked by the end of a particular alley and caught the smell of a recently lit flute. I would not look down that alley and see the person there. *I dared not.* So, I forced myself to take a few more steps, and then I stopped and just breathed while my body broke out in sweat. I almost turned around at that point. But my more reasonable mind said that would be idiotic.

I had come that far, what was a block more?

My pounding heart settled; my breathing calmed. I took another step away. Then another and another until I was myself again. But it was certainly a relief when I finally got to the street where the KG Indian market lived. I resolved to take the long way home after my little errand as well. I had passed that little test. But I saw no reason to tempt Fate a second time. I heard she could be a real bitch when she wanted.

Karun's store catered to the *Hindi*, *Sikh*, and/or *Muslim* that lived in this neighbourhood. But it also kept a good selection of western food choices and preferences as well. I found that inordinately pleasing. I knew that some specialty store owners were not so accommodating in their supply. I made a mental note to shop here more often, and tell Aurora, my Wicca roommate about it as well.

"Mr Miles! It is so nice to see you." Aruna, in her plain working clothes, came from around the counter and gathered my hands with her small, soft ones. "Is there something that I can help you find?"

"I'm not sure. I'm trying to expand my tastes a little. But I'm not ready for extremely spicy food just yet. Can you suggest something to try?"

I didn't realize until I said it, that this was an actual truth. Of late, I had found my food choices more than a little boring. So, Aruna took me around the store, pointing to this or that. It all sounded very interesting. And very tasty.

"Great. The only problem is that I have no idea how to cook that properly." I admitted, laughing at myself.

"And honestly, I'm not exactly stellar chef material."

She looked at me and smiled, "*Just a second*" and she left me standing there looking at the cans in my basket in confusion.

"Aadishree. Come watch the store for a minute, while I take Mr. Myles upstairs, please."

"Of course, Mama. Will Papa return soon?"

"He promised he would be home in time for supper. If you see Junaid, would you tell him there are chores to be done?" and with a swish of her skirt, Aruna returns. "*Please. Come.*" and she leads me upstairs to the living quarters above the store.

In her tiny kitchen, she directs me to sit and then retrieves a box from under the counter.

She begins to go through them, looking for something.. a recipe perhaps that would be simple enough for me to make.

"You are a good man, Mr. Myles. To come all this way for the sake of my husband and my son," she says without looking up from her search. "I have been married to Karun Gupta for many years. I know his heart better even than he sometimes. I know he worries about Junaid. I know he dislikes the boys that he socializes with. But I fear there is little that anyone can do in this instance. I love my husband a great deal. But his eyes refuse to see what his heart sees. Or perhaps it is the heart that does not see. He loves his son a great deal and has many plans for him. It is a pity that we were only graced with one son. Had there been two, perhaps.... things would be different. *Ah.* Here we are. A recipe for you to try. The next time we are at the House of Enlightenment, I will ask how this cooking experiment went." She offered me the recipe and smiled warmly at me.

So, I returned to the store proper and had Aadishree ring in my choices. All set to go; I turn and just coming inside is Junaid. His hair is short and gelled into a spiky updo of some sort that I'm sure has a name, but I don't know it. He's wearing a tee and jeans, and sneakers not unlike every other teenager I'd seen. Nothing particularly odd at all. The influences of both parents are evident in the face, beginning to lose that last bit of soft baby roundness. Dark eyes presently lit with happiness and a hint of mischief, perhaps.

Through the shop windows, I could see Junaid's friends. Same basic outfit as him, but they have added studded chokers and some serious black eyeliner to the whole get up. "*It suits them.*"

I think. A moment more and another, older boy joins the little group. A flashier version of the others, with studded earrings and chains instead of a choker. He speaks to the others, and as a group they share a cigarette from the older boys' proffered pack. I know this boy/man. Have seen him before working the streets, offering the one thing he has to give to those who want it. For a price.

 I glance at Junaid, and I see the light of longing in his liquid eyes. And confusion and a loneliness that should be alien to one so young.

The little lightbulb of realization flickered on. "Ah!!" I think to myself.

"Mama said you have chores to do Junaid." Aadishree says in that superior older sister tone.

Junaid answers with something in Hindi. I couldn't understand it, but I'm pretty sure I can guess what he said, and it had nothing to do with his mother or the chores. Smiling, I leave the store and take the long route home. It gave me time to sort out the various impressions I got from Junaid, his friends and Aruna's cryptic comments. I didn't have a definitive answer by the time I got there. But I could make a few educated guesses. And it also meant that I had some reading to do, before I talked to Karun again.

Was there anything that we could do at the H.O.E. to facilitate things?

I spent the next few days reading. Everything from John's notes on his time in India to studies on the Hindu religion as a whole. There was good news and bad news. I ended up going to the Hindu temple and speaking to the *Pandit Sharma* there.

Surprisingly, he had heard of the House of Enlightenment through some of his devotees, had even come and met with John a few times over the years. They had got on well, he said, and was grateful that it would open its doors to those of other faiths so they might have a safe place to worship in the smaller things. He noted that they all made the journey to the Temple for the more prominent ceremonies, so he was content, if not thoroughly happy about it.

He listened patiently to my concerns for Karun and his son. But sadly, there was no ceremony that could do what I thought needed done.

"That does not mean however, that there cannot be a pageant to create the same effect. But it will take some time to arrange and organize."

I thanked the man and returned home, hoping I had done the right thing.

Would this pageant heal or harm? I really had no way of knowing.

A few weeks later, I received a letter and an invitation to join the Pandit and the people of the *"Temple of Brahma"* in a pageant that had not been seen since the *"Ancient Homelands"* were colonized. Please feel free to invite as many of my own people as I would like, as this was a celebratory pageant for all.

I don't think even the Pandit could appreciate how quickly word passes through certain communities. By the time I arrived (and I am never late), the temple and grounds were full to bursting. I had to park several blocks away and run quickly to be on time for the beginning. As luck (if you believe in luck and coincidence) would have it, I ended up standing fairly close to *Karun* and *Aruna* and their children.

Everyone around me chatted and talked and wondered what this new pageant would be about. It was said that there had been a lot of preparation inside the temple, but those who were helping had been sworn to secrecy.

A gong sounded, and everyone grew still.

The Pandit, in full ceremonial robes, stepped forward.

"Long and long ago, the God Rama gathered his people at the edge of the forest and explained to them that he must leave for a time to perform labours. Therefore, he bid all the men and women to return to their homes and their lives until he could return to them. All but a few did as he asked. These few, who were neither man nor woman, remained at the edge of the forest for fourteen years. When Lord Rama returned and saw the faithful that had remained, he was pleased and gave these hijras powers to give blessings to the people."

A blue-painted man in head headdress and colourful loincloth stepped forward and began to chant and dance around a small group of people, their faces carefully hidden behind gauze coverings. Gradually, they began to join in the dancing with their deity, and slowly the layers of cloth and gauze came off until they were revealed in all their beauty.

Painted faces, kohl rimmed eyes, painted lips, glittering gowns, bright gold piercings, long hair in bejewelled nets or streaming loose, these men and women danced to celebrate their joy in life, their freedom. Slowly, they moved off the staged area and made their way towards the crowds, which parted and clapped for them, even as the dancers threw "rupees" into the crowd. Sometimes they would take the hand of this woman or that man and invite them to join in the dancing. One of the lucky invitees was Junaid.

Aruna watched proudly as her son moved amongst the dancers. Karun seemed resigned. For his part, Junaid was ecstatic!! When, after a time, the dancers had returned to their place on the stage, the Pandit continued his sermon:

"So, it was for a very long time. All was in harmony, and nature was happy. The people of India sought moksha and it was good. The hijras among us were revered and respected. For their ways were natural to them as your ways are natural to you. But then something changed and it was sad. The hijras were no longer demi-gods among us, they were feared and thought evil. They had to live a half-life or no life at all."

At which point the dancers sank to the floor, cowering in fear and begging for scraps from any who walked by.

No longer, though. Once more, Vishnu the Protector is happy. His avatar Lord Rama is happy. Here at least, the hijras are free once more. They no longer need to hide. Or beg. Or sell themselves. *It is good.*

"The Goddess Bahuchara Mata looks down from the Heavens."

There is an explosion of flowers. Here and there among the throng people that I hadn't noticed threw off their concealments and as with the first they began a slow sinuous dance as they weaved through the multitude, making their way slowly to the stage where a flower strewn idol waited to be picked up and carried in a great circle around the temple. The celebration went on for a few more hours of course. *Hijeras* and other members of the LGBTQ community circulated among the throng, which seemed to be mostly accepting of the differences.

A few, straight-faced and stiff, opted to leave. I guess you can't please everyone.

Satisfied, I left.

I am told that, after they got home, Junaid and his father sat down and had a long chat. I hope everything in the Gupta household is peaceful now. Not totally certain that I would like to be Aadishree, though. As eldest daughter, she's next on the list...and Karun Gupta is a determined man.

***

Adult rule 3,687...

Not all things need to be handled by *G.A.'s*

Tale 11: Chelsea

My days are reasonably simple. I get up, look after Lennie, my dog, go to one of my other part-time jobs, come home, look after Rennie. It's nice. It's peaceful. No more worrying and fretting about a place to sleep, food to eat, or warmth. It's all here in my little apartment. With a door that locks to keep me safe. I still have anxiety attacks where every little noise outside or in the hall makes my heart race. But they are getting less and less as I get more comfortable with this new life. This new me.

My social worker says that I've come a long way from the person that she first met at the House. She says I should be proud of everything that I've accomplished in the last few months. She wants me to seriously consider moving out of this neighbourhood, though. I suppose I could. But something in me isn't ready, may never be ready, to make that leap into the unknown. I've lived around here my whole life. Even when my life was "*Kip*", I still wasn't that far from my new home.

Plus, this is where the *H.O.E.* is, and I owe them a huge debt of gratitude for everything they've done or helped me do. So, if I stay, maybe I can return the favour somehow with other people who need direction. Like, I did with Petey and Gina. Here in the silence of my mind, I can admit that going out to that old warehouse was terrifying. As soon as we were on our way, I went into stealth mode. I guess old habits die hard. But that was what kept me alive in the back alleys for so long.

We. Rennie, who never leaves my side, me and that other Person, whoever she is. She calls me "*Sis*" when she talks to me, and I'm not sure she knows that I can see and hear her. And I'm not going to mention it to anybody either. The last thing I need is people thinking, I'm totally bonkers.

Especially Myles, the guy who looks after the House now that John has gone. He's kinda sweet-looking with his shaggy hair. He has the most amazing eyes too, bright green and sparkly sort of, because they have these little gold flecks in there. He's never done or said much to me, but whenever we are there at the same time, I watch him. He's buddies with Ramon. The cop that was there when my mom died.

I should hate him for that, for being the guy who called Children's Services and got me put in those foster homes. But I can't. I know he was just doing his job. And there's no way that I would have survived on the streets at eight years old. Besides, he's actually a nice guy, and some of the stuff he's seen and had to do have almost wrecked him on the inside.

But Myles and the team are helping him get better.

If the church bigwigs shut it down, I don't know what's going to happen to everyone. Nobody says much. But you can tell that they are all thinking about it. Not as happy a place as it used to be. Which sucks. I hope it all gets fingered soon.

I look at the little clock on the wall. It says 8:30. I feel sort of restless suddenly. The book I've been reading doesn't look appealing, and I don't feel like a cup of tea, so, "Hey buddy. Wanna go for a walk?" It's a silly question. Because he always wants to go for a walk. He wants to be wherever I am. He pouts when I leave him at home.

Such a sweet little nutbar, with his stubby tail and bristly face.

A few minutes later, the pair of us is walking down the street. It's not dark enough for the street lights yet. There are still lots of people around, doing their shopping or going home to work. It will be a while yet before the nightlife takes over. So, I feel reasonably safe. Besides, Rennie will warn me if anybody seems odd to him.

We don't really have an actual destination in mind. But our steps seem to be heading in the general direction of the House. I wonder if Myles is still there or has, he gone home for the night? I can't remember which nights he runs the AA meetings. As I walk, I see a few people I recognize, either from work or the House. We smile and nod at each other and carry on. It occurs to me that, for me, this is a novel experience. I used to try so very hard not to be seen or recognized. If they know you, they could follow you. If they follow you, they could hurt you. Better to hide or not be seen at all.

I started humming some little nonsense song as I walked.

It's funny how perspectives change......

A few steps later, Rennie and I rounded a corner. Up ahead, I can see the warm lights of the H.O.E. Shining through the stained-glass windows, welcoming and soft. Like a hug that I wasn't aware I needed until I saw it. I passed an alley... one that I've walked by before. Suddenly, there's a beefy arm around my neck and a hard voice warning me not to scream... not that I could because the arm was cutting off my air. My heart began to race. I gulped for whatever air I could get, which wasn't much. Everything started to get hazy around the edges, and tears were streaming from my eyes.

I tried clawing at the arm, I tried kicking, I threw my head backwards, hoping to hit him in the nose. But it did me no good. He was just too big and strong. Inch by inch, he dragged me backwards. Into the alley where there was no light at all. Rennie came running. Barking for all he was worth. But the man paid no attention to my little mutt, until he felt the needles of teeth in the flesh of his calf. *Helpless*, I watched as he lashed out with a heavy boot. Rennie slammed against the wall and stopped moving.

I hoped he was just stunned. If anything happened to my best friend in the whole world.....

Terrified for Rennie and myself, I fought some more. Blood was streaming freely from the scratches I had made. But it didn't bother him any more than my attempts to get free did. The arm around my throat might as well have been a band of steel for all the effect I was having. Slowly, the air in my lungs was leaking away, and with it my consciousness. My legs gave out, and my attacker half-carried me further into the alley. Sure, that I was beyond fighting anymore, the pressure on my throat eased as he threw me into a pile of rags behind some structure. I dragged in a much-needed breath.

The next instant, he was on top of me, pulling at my top and my bra, then the snaps on my jeans. I could smell the sour stench of his breath, feel the thick fingers pinching at my skin as he tore away my clothes, and see the thin lips stretched over stained teeth. His eyes were bottomless black pits.

From somewhere, he produced a knife, and the stubborn denim buttons and material gave way. Then pain and hoarse laughter, and merciful blackness.

***

Ramon and I were standing outside the *H.O.E.* The meeting was over for the night, all the others had left. It was quiet. By rights, we should have gone home ourselves. But neither of us felt like moving. It was Ramon who saw him first. A small shadow on the sidewalk, dragging himself along painfully slowly.

"What's that?" he wondered as he dropped the butt of his smoke in the can.

Curious, but not cautious, he moved towards it. I followed. Seconds later, we could see that it was a tiny dog, patchy white fur caked in blood and filth, but still his nubbin of a tail wagged once when he saw us. Then he collapsed. I ran to Rennie. Ramon ran to his car to get a flashlight. We both knew that the little dog was never far from Chelsea's side. He was alive. But barely. I stripped off my shirt and wrapped the poor critter in it as carefully as I could. He never even whimpered.

All the while I was thinking furiously, "Melody!! Something has happened to Chelsea! We need to find her! Fast."

Not even a block away, I saw Melody step out of an alley, agitated, running in and out, until she was sure I had seen her. Ramon and I followed the trail the pooch had made. The blood smears he left behind looked ghastly in the light of the torch. I could just imagine how horrible he would look in the light. I tried really hard not to think about what we would find in that alley.

***

I wasn't doing anything specific when I heard Myles scream my name, just checking on a few people that I'd been watching. In the blink of an eye, I found her. *Half-naked.* Covered in bruises and blood but still alive. I was relieved, until I saw the figure in the shadows, waiting patiently.

"Oh NONONONO!" I cry out as I kneel by her side.

"Come on, Sis! Hang in there. Myles is coming! He'll get you to the hospital! But you gotta hang on. Don't go on me! Not yet."

A breathy whisper of "No. Not Myles." and then Chelsea is silent once more.

How could I have let this happen?

How could this even happen without me knowing?

To my own sister?

How good am I going to be as a Guardian if I can't even protect my own damn sister?

I held her hand, sort of, and placed the palm of my other hand over her heart so I could feel it beating. I did my level best to ignore the dark shadow still waiting in the corner. He hasn't moved. Hasn't said a word. I couldn't even tell if it was my D or not.

And there I waited until Myles and Ramon arrived.

***

I see Melody arrive. See her go immediately to her sister. Know it the moment that she notices me waiting there. Though it hurts like the dickens, because I know exactly how she is feeling right then, I can't go over there and console her. Can't interfere.

I wait.

***

Ramon and I turn the corner. I see Melody kneeling by a still form in the garbage and refuse.

"Is she still alive?" I think of the wavering form, crying silently.

"Yes," she answers without taking her eyes away.

"Ramon! Call an ambulance. She's still alive." I say to the man beside me.

But he is already on his cell, calling for ambulances and scene techs. I set my wrapped bundle down and kneel beside Chelsea's still form, unknowingly mimicking the position of her sister in doing so. A whimper escapes from the bundle and from Chelsea.

***

I watch, horrified, as D steps out of the shadows. Thank the *PTB*, it is my D and not one of the others. Calmly, he steps over to where Myles and I are huddled, looks down at the three of us, sad but resolute. He reaches out his big hand and gently unwraps the bundle that Myles had been carrying. With a whispered word, Rennie floats free of the cloth and the pain and the sorrow.

He had done what he needed to do. His person was in safe hands now. He could go.

I whisper "Thank you" as the two depart. I'm not sure if I was thanking the dog or thanking D for not taking my sister. I don't suppose it really matters.

***

I have no idea how many days later it is when I finally wake up. I can tell immediately that I am in a hospital. There are machines everywhere around me, making soft beeping noises. There are things stuck in my arms, and I am wrapped in bandages. And I hurt everywhere. The lights are dim. But I can see a couple of chairs pulled close to my bedside. One is empty. Myles is sitting in the other holding his head in his hands. He's wearing a T-shirt and jeans, which I've never seen him in before. His hair is a mess, like he's been running his hands through it, and there is the shadow of whiskers on his chin.

If it weren't for the circumstances and my own condition, I might have found the whole picture rather appealing. But I remembered her telling me that Myles was coming. So, he had seen me after. Which made the fact that he was here even more amazing. Also, a lot more uncomfortable.

"Hey," I croaked.

He shot out of the chair like it was on fire, reached out and grabbed my hand. Were his hands shaking? He smiled, and it lit up his whole face, the eyes especially.

"Hey, yourself," he answers.

"How are you feeling?" he brushes a stray strand of hair away from my face.

"Dunno yet. Sore."

It was the only thing I could think of to say. Then I remembered, "Ren?" I asked.

The bright green eyes lost their shine. He looked at me and shook his head.

"He managed to live long enough to come get help, though. He was a brave little dude."

Then I cried. And Myles held me, and we cried some more.

When I was stronger, a police officer came to see me. She took my statement. Asked questions that I could answer and questions I couldn't. She told me that they had taken samples from under my nails and the rest of me, and that was all logged as evidence for when they caught the guy. Did I think I would be able to identify him if I ever saw him again?

Honestly, I'm not sure. Because of the choke hold, everything has a hazy, unreal appearance in my memory. Or maybe I just don't want to remember. They had to give me sleeping pills the night before because I had woken up screaming and couldn't calm down. Myles came to see me every day. A few of the other women did as well. I felt very cosseted by everyone. And maybe a little smothered as well. Which made me mad at myself. They were only being their usual nice selves. I was the one being uncharitable.

What am I supposed to be feeling?

What is normal in a situation like this?

Even worse is that this isn't the first time… It is all very confusing.

Going home is particularly hard. As soon as I open the door, I expect to hear a happy little yip. But of course, there isn't one. There is his food and his dishes to remind me that he has been here. There is his favourite toy stuck under my pillow, waiting. For a little guy to come squeak it and interrupt my sleep. But he never will again. The pain in my heart is unbearable in those first days. The memories are joy and sorrow so interwoven I can't tell the difference.

And in feeling that I don't have to take the time to deal with my own horrors.

Until nighttime. When sane people sleep.

And there he is, all fetid breath and fathomless eyes, waiting for me to step past that alley.

I haven't had the courage to go for a walk since I got out of the hospital.

***

I am pissed. More at myself than anything. But I want to do something, anything, that will help me feel less guilty about being totally unaware of my own sister being attacked and raped! Strangely though, I can't step into her mind and draw out the images of the attacker. Somehow, she's managed to close that off. Even in the hospital. Which is where I first tried it. John is conspicuously absent right now as well, which doesn't really make me feel any better. I want to spend as much time as possible with Chelsea. But with him gone, I have a lot more people to look after, so to speak, than I usually do. So, I flash in when I can.

Every time I do, she flinches a little.

Odd.

I hate feeling so helpless.

***

It's been a couple of weeks. I have to go to work. The bills and the rent still have to be paid. All the outward signs of my attack have faded. There are no visible scars to tell that anything happened to me at all. But getting dressed seems to take forever. My muscles are molasses. My heart is beating triple time and I am having a hard time catching my breath. Every little thing that isn't working like it should seems like the universe telling me to stay at home. Hide. For a little longer. Or until the rest of the world forgets you even existed.

Almost.

Almost I gave in and decided to stay at home.

It would be so much easier.

But then there is a knock on the door.

Shaking and petrified, I force myself to open the door a crack.

Myles is standing there. Clean-shaven and neatly combed. Dressed in his familiar white button-down and slacks.

"Hi," he says, smiling.

"Hi yourself," I answer, opening the door wider. But not too wide.

"I heard from Aurora that you were coming into work today. I thought I'd stop by. See if you want a walking buddy."

"Oh. Gee. Thanks." I say, while thinking to myself, "Well nuts."

Having no other option now, I gather my purse and jacket, lock the apartment door, and together we step out into the bright morning sunshine. It feels good to have that warmth on my face again. To see the trees up close instead of through a window. To have the breeze teasing my hair as it wanders by.

But as we stroll along, there is a little voice in the back of my head that asks, "Can she tell? Can he see?" every time we walk by someone and they look directly at me.

The same little voice that says "He's just being nice because he feels sorry for you. You're damaged goods now. He's seen the damaged goods. He will never be anything more. I don't see it, but little by little as we trudge along, I am shrinking deeper and deeper into myself until finally Myles takes my arm and we stop".

"Chelsea." he says, so very gently that I want to cry, "It's not your fault. The attack was a thing that happened to you. Not because you wanted it to. Not because you deserved it or anything. Not for any reason other than the fact that you were in the wrong place at the wrong time. It doesn't change who you are. It doesn't make any of US feel any different about you. It doesn't matter to us, except that it's making you so miserable and unhappy. We want to see you smile again. We want, hell, I want to see you happy again. Please. Help us. Meet us halfway. If you need to see someone to help you, that's fine. I'll help you find them. Or your worker will. But we really need you to come back to us," gently, stroking my cheek where a bruise was not so awfully long ago.

"Please."

What can I say?

What can I promise?

"I'll try." I mumble while unshed tears gather in my lashes.

Hand in hand we continue down the street.

Tale 12: Good Samaritan

Sighing and more than a little sad, I lay the drop sheet over the still face and step back so the CS guys and the coroner can do their thing. My partner and I begin a meticulous search of the immediate area, hoping something will stand out among the effluvia. But neither of us were holding out much hope. This scene didn't seem to be any different than the other three that we had already been to in the last month. Another homeless, nameless person was stabbed to death in the city by a person or persons unknown. No weapon, no clues. No, nothing to point us in the direction of the perpetrator. The only commonalities the fact that they were indigents, with no fixed address. Therefore, easy targets.

The bodies appeared to be abandoned in a place removed from the original crime scene as well, judging by the lack of blood and traces at each scene. So, the perp had a vehicle of some kind. In my mind, I ventured to guess that the DBs were being left closer and closer to the House of Enlightenment. But that was just a guess. Not something I could put in my report. So, I had to stick to the script, interview locals, and the person who found him. Yada, yada, yada. Even knowing ahead of time that this was probably going to be a dry hole. Off book, on my own time, I could possibly answer questions and hope it gave us a lead of some sort.

Georgi and Myles might know more than they realize. Georgi, because she had lived a good portion of her life on these streets and knew a lot of people here still. People who might be more willing to talk to her than me, passing along rumours that I might not hear otherwise. Myles, as the de facto head of the House, might be able to identify the three victims, if they had ever used the House for anything. He might even know of anybody suspicious in the area.

And what might the *H.O.E.* have to do with the attacks? Assuming that they are being left for a reason. So, after my shift ended, I pulled up in front of the brick building. Everything seemed to be business as usual. People coming and going, parcels going in, parcels going out. Cars coming, cars going. People walking, head up and confident, others sliding along like they don't want to be noticed.

I catalogue the details of the ones I don't recognize, watching where they go, or what vehicle they drive, until I can't see them anymore; wishing I had thought to bring a camera, forgetting, naturally, that there is one there on my cell until it's too late. Wishing that I had something to drink besides water, knowing that feeling will never leave me, and squashing it back into its little drawer. Almost like he knew I was there, Myles steps out and leans casually against the door jamb.

I like the guy.

But something about him is a little—odd. He sometimes knows things he shouldn't. Maybe he's just a good guesser. Maybe he's one of those people who can read body language as easily as I read the newspaper. Dunno. And I really don't have the time to figure it out anyway.

***

I am sitting in the office rewriting, for the hundredth time, a proposal to send to the Diocese regarding St. Therese when John "popped" in. I mean, not literally. They don't "pop" exactly. But they can and do randomly show up. Sometimes, like now, for instance, I can see him or Melody as a hazy, indistinct presence. Mostly, though, they just show up as a voice in my head.

"Good afternoon, John."

I thought speaking out loud was being unnecessary and more than a little unnerving to an accidental observer.

"Myles," he answered as he casually wandered around the office.

He said nothing further, but continued to wander, stopping finally in front of a framed photo on the wall to my left. I saved my work and shut down the laptop.

"Ramon is coming," he says, casually.

"Oh?" I answer.

It wasn't a meeting day, so maybe he was having a bad day and trying really hard not to drink? Or maybe it was something else.

"Georgianna will be here shortly." John adds.

"Okay." So not an AA thing probably at all. They would not be coming to me for relationship advice. So definitely something else. If John knew, he obviously wasn't telling. So.. I would wait. Oh well. I wasn't getting anywhere with the proposal anyway.

Time for a quick smoke?

***

We saw Georgianna coming down the sidewalk, so Myles and I waited so the three of us could enter together. We went to the office immediately, not bothering to chat with any of the other patrons as we went by. I wasn't sure how exactly to begin and express my concerns and suspicions, so it took me a minute to organize my thoughts. Myles and Georgianna waited patiently. They both know me fairly well, so they knew what I was doing, even if they had no clue what the problem may be.

"Georgi, have you heard anything from your friends in the last few months? Is there anybody new on the street that people are wondering about?" I ask.

Georgi tilts her head a little, considering all the incident rumours and whatnot that she hears at the shelter where she works. A small frown puckers her forehead as she mentally sorts through all the little bits and pieces.

"Sorry Ray. Nothing that I can think of. There's the usual gossip about dealers and pimps and who got hurt by who. But nothing I would consider strange."

"Myles. You heard anything? See anything? Strangers coming into the House that seem over interested in the homeless?"

"No. Why? Something going on?" he asks, leaning forward now, eyes intent and curious.

So, I'll explain briefly about the three murders we've had in the precinct in the last month. Explain that it is our belief that they are killed and then transported to this area.

"Has the House gotten any letters or unusual mail lately? Something that might seem threatening, even in a marginal sense."

Myles reaches across the desk and retrieves a stack of mail from a box in the corner. "This is all the mail we've received in the last two weeks. I've been busy trying to write a proposal for the church, so I haven't read any of it yet. As near as I can recall, there wasn't anything in the weeks before that, though. Just the usual stuff."

"Okay."

The next few minutes, we busied ourselves going through the small stack of letters. Flyers of any kind that looked normal, we ignored. Nothing weird popped out at us, though. So that was a dead end.

"Why would the *H.O.E.* get threatening letters?" Myles asked after we were done.

"Well, this is just a theory. But everybody we find seems to be left closer to the House every time. Like the killer is trying to send a message. To whom and why, I have no idea. He doesn't give us much to go on. So right now, I'm just working from theory and suspicions at this point. We've been canvassing the area around the drop sites, but nobody sees anything. Or so they say. But you both know how hard it is to get people to talk to the cops. They are as afraid of us as they are of the bad guys. That's why I asked about local rumours. I was hoping somebody said something in passing that got your attention. But if nothing else, you can warn the homeless around you that there's someone using them as target practice. I would appreciate it if you hear anything, you will let me know."

Myles offered Georgi and me coffee, but we both politely declined. As there wasn't anything else to discuss, we both left the *H.O.E.*

She was kind enough to accept my offer of a ride home, due to the lateness of the hour.

The day started out crappy. But I hoped it would end in one of the best ways possible. I think anyway. Not being an aficionado of the female mind, I can only suppose. And she isn't saying much. She does, however, snore—in a very lady-like way.

***

I watched the pair leave, trying hard not to react to Ramon's courtly manners as he held Georgi's elbow down the stairs and opened the car door for her as well. Then I went back to the office. Neither had been aware of his presence through the entire discussion, but John had been there listening. In fact, it was still there waiting for me. "Well," I said as I closed the door.

"Yes. Very troubling," he replies calmly.

"Any thoughts on who it might be?" I ask, knowing already that if he answered, it was liable to be cryptic and vague.

"None that I can offer at the moment. But Ramon is right. As many people as possible need to be informed. Just in case his suspicions are indeed fact."

"You are right, of course." I agree. I check my watch. In an hour or so, the nightly visitors would start arriving.

"I'll start on that as they come in. Discretely, of course. In the meantime, I had best let Deacon Baderhoff know what's happening."

I walk over and begin to reach for the phone.

"Oh, I wouldn't bother Robert just yet. Time enough for that later." John says.

Not that it really bothered me not to speak to the Deacon, because personally I think he's a supercilious prig, but I did wonder at the odd, hard tone in John's voice. It was also strange because generally, John believes that the man should be told about darn near everything that happens in the House. As he often reminds me, technically, it is still St. Therese and the Catholic Church. I looked at the hazy figure standing beside the old photo, but made no comment.

Neither did he. Surprise. Surprise.

***

The next few days were typical, except that now we made a point of gently asking names and writing down brief descriptions of every person who borrowed our floor space for the night, or used the little tented area out back. Whenever possible, we got permission and took pictures. Chelsea was a huge help in this. I had forgotten how she came to the House, and it never occurred to me that she might personally know some of these people and be in "contact" with them still. I hesitated to ask her for help in the first place because of her own attack earlier in the year. She says I'm being overprotective. It's a little hard not to be. I can still see her lying in the filth, *broken* and *bleeding*. As near as we could tell, there didn't seem to be anyone missing. But it's difficult to say for certain, as it is a rather fluid existence, and the same people do not show up every night. Georgi, I assume, is experiencing the same difficulties where she works for the same reasons. Not to mention the sheer number of homeless people that are out there on any given night.

But we kept records as best we were able, no matter how frustrating we found it to be. No news from Ramon either on how the investigation was going. Or whether the murders did in fact, have something to do with our little safe haven. John and Melody both were conspicuously absent. Or obnoxiously silent through the whole affair.

***

"Four days." I think to myself as I drive my old sedan around the teeming streets. Streets that I drive so often, I am sure the car operates on autopilot. In the back seat is a box full of sandwiches and fruit. At the next corner, I will stop and start doling out the food to whoever is there to take it. This also is a routine that is familiar to me and the wretched souls that receive my largess. The usual people will be there waiting for me, I'm sure. They are rather like trained dogs that way. Which is convenient. It saves time, and they are less likely to say anything to the authorities because the easy source of food might dry up. That is assuming any of them are smart enough to suspect anything. *Which I doubt*.

I stopped the car against the curb. As if by magic, as soon as I open the back door, there come all my puppies, eager to be fed and petted and told how wonderful they are in the eyes of God. Tonight, when I get home, I will burn the clothes that I'm wearing and scrub myself raw in a scalding shower to remove the stench and disease. And in four days, one puppy will have a rather severe stomach ailment, and, good Samaritan that I am, I will take that poor soul someplace to get help.

"Because the poor are plundered, because the needy groan, I will now arise. I will place him in the safety for which he longs."

- Psalm 12:5

***

I could tell at that week's meeting that there were still no clues from Ramon's tense posture as he sat in his chair listening as other members shared their stories. He was as close to breaking as I had ever seen him. Not since that first meeting had he looked at the gathering with cop eyes, but he was doing it now.

Could the killer actually be someone from inside the House?

Someone who was here regularly for meetings?

Someone less directly involved, perhaps?

I hate the idea that it might be. But who knows what lies buried in a person's secret heart?

The only ones who might be able to answer that weren't saying much at the moment.

Frustration is rapidly becoming a familiar feeling of late.

After the actual meeting was over, we three had a brief conference of our own to compare notes, so to speak. I was right. There are still no leads on the case, and Ramon is afraid that apathy towards the victims might shut it down almost entirely. But at the moment he is doing his best to get to the bottom of it. I handed him the folder of people that we managed to catalogue thus far and was about to wish him good hunting but there was a commotion at the front door.

"Help! Somebody, please, help!" a man cried out, even as he struggled through the entryway carrying a body close to his chest.

Both are covered in blood, bright scarlet stains spreading rapidly across the ragged clothes of the unconscious victim and the starched white shirt of the man carrying him. The cloying iron stench of it was almost my undoing as I felt my stomach contents rise to the back of my throat.

Fortunately, Ramon and Georgianna are made of sterner stuff. Ramon took the victim and laid him on the parquet flooring and checked for a pulse. Georgi whipped out her cell and called 911. I finally found the presence of mind to lead the man out of the way and sit him down in a chair. He is so pale, eyes wide and stunned looking, I had visions of him passing out before Ramon had time to ask any questions.

I sent one of the helpers to fetch him a glass of water, another to get clean towels, and a basin of water. The man's hands are covered in blood, and he's smeared it across his face in the stress of the moment.

In fact, it isn't until he is nominally clean again that I see who it actually is.

“Deacon Baderhoff! I'm sorry, Sir. I didn't recognize you when you came in.” I said, taking the bloody towel from his shaking hands and setting it carefully on a plastic bag.. (The girl who brought the towel must have known and brought the plastic with her to preserve the evidence, for which I silently thanked her for her initiative.)

“No, Myles. It's alright. I'm not the Deacon. Robert is my brother. I'm Roger.”

“Oh! I'm sorry again. I didn't realize that he had a brother. You look an awful lot alike.” I started noticing the small differences then.

“Well, we are twins. So, I suppose that's not unusual,” he smiles slightly.

“Not technically identical. But twins all the same.”

His eyes, calmer now, begin to travel around the room. Every now and then, a small frown puckers his forehead, there and gone so quickly that it might never have been there at all. Never once does he turn to look at Ramon as he does whatever he's doing to the wounded man on the floor.

Moments later, the EMTs and the police arrive to take over from Ramon.

Have you ever noticed that in highly stressful situations, time seems to stretch and you begin to notice every little detail about every little thing? I have never had that happen to me before, but as Ramon strode over, his own clothes now gore-stained, I stepped back and observed.

More closely than I would have thought possible. The dirt on the tips of Roger's shoes and the cuffs of his pants. The pattern of blood on his pants and his shirt. The way he is sitting in the chair as Ramon asks his questions. The expression on his face when Ramon mentions the victim, the lack of emotion in his eyes. Something isn't quite adding up. But I have no idea what it is. Something is off kilter here.

"Will he make it?" Roger asks as the victim is taken away to the ambulance.

Am I imagining it, or did Roger sound a little nervous?

"The ambulance guys think so. The wounds weren't as severe as they looked. The guy had a lot of padding between him and the knife blade. And since you got him here so fast after the attack, his chances are even better." Ramon says while he writes in his notepad.

"Good. That's good." Roger says, standing up.

"Now, if you'll excuse me, I really want to go home and change."

"Sure. I'll follow behind." Ramon states, in his "cop" voice.

"Really, officer. I hardly think that's necessary."

"Yup, it is. Your clothes might have traces on them from where you picked up the victim. I need to collect them for the CS guys."

Ramon looks up from his notes. "Is that a problem?"

"No. No problem at all. I just never Thought of that." Roger says calmly enough. But Ramon and I can both see him gritting his teeth.

"Come to think of it, we will probably need the car too. So, I guess we will go to the station instead. There should be something there that we can slip you into. And then I can run you home." The smile he directed at Roger is supposed to be reassuring.

But Roger doesn't look like he is getting it. At all.

Melody and John both chose that second to make a brief appearance. Hard eyed, they stare at Roger, who is fidgeting a little. Reaction for what reason?

I am still thinking about it all, trying to sort it out as Ramon leads Roger away.

The CS people are still doing their thing up front. I take them the baggie with the bloody towel. If for no other reason than because I don't want to look at it anymore. They tag it and set it in the paper sacks of stuff collected so far. I desperately want a smoke.

But first, I have to reassure all the House people that "Everything is fine. If we don't get the mess cleaned up tonight, we can cover it with an old rug if necessary, until tomorrow morning. In the meantime, there really wasn't anything else to do, so if they wanted, they were free to go home."

Then I escaped out the back door. Where I breathed in the fresh, city-scented air with relief. My stomach settled.

Melody joined me. "Better now?"

She leans casually against the door frame. Since the door is still open, I can't answer verbally. It's been a strange enough evening. The last thing the helpers need is to see me talking to myself. But my mind is occupied by all the impressions it needs to organize into some semblance of coherence, so I don't think the answer either. And really, there was no need.

"Be sure and tell Ray that he needs to check Will's jacket pockets. Thoroughly."

Melody tells me and then leaves me to have my smoke in peace.

Rather than call, I texted the name of the victim and Melody's message to Ramon, ending with, "Will explain later," to forestall the millions of questions that would be created, and hoped that would be enough for now.

I lit my smoke, and as I exhaled, I let my body relax and began going through the images in my head, one at a time. There was definitely something there. Niggling at me like a loose tooth. But every time I thought I was close, it slipped away. It became an exercise in frustration.

Apparently, my idea of later and Ramon's were more than slightly different. He showed up about an hour later, while I was getting the cleaning supplies together that I was likely to need.

No warm up at all as he walked in the door, "Ok. Explain."

"You're gonna think I'm crazy. Or stoned. Because there really isn't any way that I can prove what I'm about to tell you." I said as I carried rags and bleach to the front.

"Don't care. I need to know how you knew about the sandwich in his pocket. And the rest of it."

"Jeez. You lead with the tough ones don't you."

He gave me a look as he grabbed thick gloves and more rags.

"You don't have to help clean up, you know." I said as I knelt down.

"Nope. Now answer the damn question."

So together Ramon and I cleaned up the blood and the dirt and the dusting powder and the little bits of stuff. And I talked and talked and talked. I don't think I've yakked that much since grade school.

At least not about myself.

"So.. Melody told you about the sandwich? Did she say why?" he asked in a normal tone of voice. No shrinking away or surreptitiously dialing the local mental facility.

"Uh huh, and no, she didn't."

"Are they here right now?" he looked to my left and then my right.

I was about to say no when they both popped in. "As a matter of fact, they just got here."

"Oh."

I could see him searching around in his head for the next question even as his eyes scanned the area around us. "Melody. Is there some way that you can, you know...."

"Can you make the floor soapy or something?" she asked me. So, I dipped my rag in the water and slopped some suds on the parquet. Then, as carefully as she could, she wrote, "Hi, Ray," in the bubbles and signed it with an "M".

I'm pretty sure it took every nerve Ramon had or will have, not to jump up and run screaming out of the building at that point. But I had to give the guy credit, he stayed exactly where he was as he watched the letters forming in the soapy water.

"Uh.... Hi," he choked out. And then he just sat there and stared until the letters slowly disappeared.

"Oh, hi Sis!" Melody says next, a smile spreading quickly across her face.

And now it was my turn to stiffen up in shock and then look behind me. Chelsea was walking slowly towards us, carrying two steaming cups of coffee. She was blushing furiously as she came forward.

"I'm sorry. I didn't mean to eavesdrop. I thought you might like something to drink. But the conversation was so interesting that I couldn't help myself." She set the cups down on a nearby table, which made John wince and then shrug.

"Um.... so, you can... see her? Too," she whispered, voice full of wonder.

"I'm not bonkers? She's really there?"

Oh man. This was gonna be a long ass night.

"Yes, Chelsea. I can see her." I said as I stood up.

"Oh, thank God... or whoever!" she says as she grabs hold of me, laughing and crying at the same time. How the hell do women do that? "I was so afraid that you would think I was crazy. So, I never said. And this whole time you could see her too!"

I rubbed her back and made comforting noises. Secretly enjoying the feeling of being held by this special girl. Even if the circumstances were far from ideal at the moment.

When everyone was a little calmer, I suggested that we finish cleaning up the mess and then go have a long talk in the office, where the chairs are a whole lot more comfortable than squatting on the floor.

A week after the longest (but best) night of my life, all the reports were in. It made front-page news in fact.

"According to sources within the police department, the man responsible for the deaths of four homeless persons has been identified and arrested. Roger Baderhoff, brother of Deacon Robert Baderhoff of St. Therese of the Roses Catholic Church, has been apprehended after a long and thorough investigation. Mr. Baderhoff faces four counts of murder in the first degree and, if convicted, could possibly spend the rest of his life behind bars. There is some talk that his mental state at the time of the crimes was questionable and may be sent for psychiatric evaluation before trials may begin. The first hearing and decisions are set for Tuesday next. Deacon Baderhoff and the Catholic Diocese have declined comment at this time."

The next day the news article said:

Once again accused killer Roger Baderhoff has made news. Hours before he was due to appear before Judge William Halden, Mr. Badderhoff was found deceased in his cell. He had apparently hung himself with a bed sheet. He was discovered by an officer doing his rounds.

He left behind a note that purportedly says:

I seethe with anger.

The church of my youth, bastion of decency and love is no more.

Did they think I did not see the iconography of false gods?

Barely hidden by equally false cloths?

Did they think I would not see the sadness in the eyes of St. Therese who so proudly graced the vestibule?

I am amazed that she does not bleed in her distress. Even as Our Lord bled

for the unclean and Godless.

How could they allow this infamy to happen?

How did they not rise up in protest?

I had hoped that I might make them see.

The homeless have no way to reach the Kingdom of God here.

There is no surcease for their pain.

The Church has turned a blind eye to the hand of Satan.

"All my bones shall say, Oh Lord, I am like you,

delivering the poor from him who is too strong and robs them."

But now I am lost.

I am lost.

Once again, the Diocese and Deacon Baderhoff declined comment.

The church referred to in the suicide note is "*St. Therese of the Roses*", known by its local community as "The House of Enlightenment".

Tale 13: Student of Humanity

Every day, rain or shine, I walk by the building everyone around here calls the House of Enlightenment. It's out of my way to do it, because there are shortcuts I can take instead to the bookstore where I work. I'm not even sure there is a logical answer why I take the long way around. It's just a feeling I get when I walk by and look up at the bell tower that I repaired. But it's more than just pride in a job well done. I dunno. There's a special kind of peace there, I suppose.

Maybe it has something to do with John, the old priest who used to run the place before my roommate took over. Maybe it's because all the gods and goddesses are allowed to exist there, free of criticism and persecution. I'm not quite sure how he managed it. *Whatever*. I do know that it's making a difference, though. *Somehow*.

Things just feel better now than they did when I first moved into the neighbourhood. I look around me and I see people smiling, walking with their heads up, looking me in the eye, and not as judgmental as they used to be. Well, most of them anyway. There will always be a few that see the hair and the makeup, the tats and the clothes that will assume that I am an awful person. And that's on them. They can wear their fancy clothes and perfect hair as a shield to hide the secrets that live behind closed doors, all they want. I hope for their sake they can survive it or are eventually smart enough to get help. *Or get out*.

There are also the trolls that drive down the non-residential streets and assume that I'm for sale. Or something. I have an in with the local cops, though, so I write down plate numbers and pass it along. It's a thing we all started doing when that whole thing went down with Baderhoff. We all look after our own here. Though technically he was one of us, it was a bad scene for a while. And we're more cautious about strangers. For now, anyway. Eventually, we will relax again. But in the meantime, some of us keep the cops, especially Ray, in the loop. *Just in case*.

I know, right? Makes no sense. On the one hand, I am more comfortable living here, but at the same time, I'm on alert for anything out of the ordinary. It's a weird way to do it. But I'm doing it, I know I'm doing it, I know why I'm doing it. And I can no more stop myself from doing it than I can freeze time.

It isn't logical. But who said everything is logical? Sometimes things are just because they are.

I have to wait for a walk light so I can cross. Me and ten other people that I see every day.

"Hey Aurora. How's things?" one asks me as she shifts the backpack on her shoulder.

"Hey. Not so bad. You?" I'm lousy at remembering names. Faces, I never forget, though.

"Oh, you know. SSDD," she says as she laughs lightly. "Be glad when this paper is written. Tired of lugging books around."

"Yeah sure. Then you'll be moving into the Ivory Towers across town and you'll wish you were still here, lugging books around." I laugh back.

"Yeah, maybe. But right now, I can't wait," she replies as the light turns. We cross together. She goes right. I turn left. She waves as we part company. I wave back.

I pass KG's. Business is booming by the looks of it. There are people already looking over the stuff freshly placed outside the door. The shopkeeper and his wife are beaming as customers begin to queue up. Their son and daughter are waiting patiently by the register. I promise myself I'll come back at lunch for a pita sandwich and carry on.

As I round another corner, I see Chelsea (one of the few whose name I remember, because if I didn't Myles would likely curb my ass and I'd have to find new digs). She looks better and better every day. Except for the slight flinch when she is brushed by a passing person, you'd never know what happened to her. Myles might have something to do with that. Or maybe it's Melody striding along at her side, unseen. By everybody except Chelsea. And I. *Shhhh*. That's a secret. Though one of these days, I suppose the four of us are gonna have to sit down and have a talk. Not yet, though. The whole experience of having a sister, who isn't alive, but isn't dead either, takes some adjustment.

"Hey Chels," I say as I walk past. I wink at Melody. She winks back.

"Hey Aurora," she answers back, saying nothing about the wink, maybe thinking it was for her.

The little bell over the door tinkles as I open it. I think to myself, "That is SO cliche." But honestly, I wouldn't change it. I stop for a minute and suck in a breath. Is it just me, or do bookstores have their own special smell? I couldn't begin to describe it but there is something soothing about it. *Like burning beeswax candles.* Something soft. Something patient. Something not totally of "*here*".

I know, I'm weird. Mr. B, who owns the bookstore, says that to me a lot. Especially first thing in the morning. The door was open. Where is he? He's usually here waiting for me.........Me being me, I know he isn't gone. There's no feeling that he is anywhere. But that doesn't mean he isn't hurt someplace and needs help. Worried, I stow my own backpack under the counter and start searching. Up and down the aisles I walk. Searching around every corner, behind every shelf that isn't backed to the wall. *Nothing.* Then through the back room and into the storage area, looking behind stacked boxes and miscellaneous accumulated crud. *Again nothing.*

So, the store itself is empty except for me. That leaves the apartment upstairs. To get there, I need to go out the back and up the alley stairs. It's not a long walk. The bookstore isn't humongous, but it feels like my feet are weighted with each step, like I'm walking through molasses. I know it's fear for Mr. B. dragging at me, my urge for self-preservation, trying to protect me. But I'm a big girl now. Fear can't stop me unless I let it. I push through it and the outside door simultaneously. The garbage bins are there under the stairs, lids askew, which is odd. Mr. B. is particular about the lids being on tight. Because of rats who eat books if they can. I take a step. Then another, calling out, "Mr. B? Are you there?"

At first, nothing. Then a moan from the back of the last can. And there he is. His pants are dirty. His sweater vest as well. One loafer is missing somewhere. He's sort of curled up around himself like he's in pain. But I don't see any blood. Or at least not much. There's a scrape on his cheek.

"Hey," I say softly, pulling out my cell (thank the Goddess for technology that is moveable). "You're gonna be ok. I'm calling an ambo. You're gonna be fine. Hang on, okay?" He nods slightly and moans. But doesn't speak.

It feels like forever when you're waiting for help to get to you. Time has a funny way of stretching in moments of stress. The experts will say because of the adrenaline funnelling through your system or something like that. So, forever are only a few minutes. *But it still feels like forever.* When they did show up, I told them what I knew, which wasn't much, despite the fact that I'd been his employee for two years already. Then they whisked him away. *I had to stay behind.* It just occurred to me that I hadn't locked the store. I hoped everything was okay there. And I also had to find numbers for his son and daughters. They needed to know that he was in the hospital.

A new cop on the block went with me to check out the store and then up to the apartment to find the contact info. I guess because it was his job. And I suspect my appearance made him a tad suspicious of my motivations. *Whatever.* At least the insurance guys would be happy.

So, for a day that started off with such promise, it sure dragged on. People came and went, some to buy, some to satisfy their curiosity. It helped pass the time at least. It was the end of the day before the daughter showed up. Not the nice one either. This was the one who got lucky and married money. And promptly forgot how backstreet poor she was as a kid. I can't stand her. Even a little bit. But for M. B's sake, I plastered on a fake smile and watched her sail in the door like the Queen of Sheba. Expensive perfume wafted out of her designer suit and silk scarf. Her makeup was perfect still, even though she had just spent the day at the hospital with her sick dad. She is a well-dressed mannequin that used to be a woman.

"Well. Anjelica. It seems I have you to thank for saving poor Papa this morning." It didn't sound that sincere. In fact, it almost sounded like she was annoyed.

"Is he gonna be okay?"

"Yes, fortunately. It was a heart attack. But not a severe one, thank goodness. He will be out of the hospital in a few days. I have the best cardiac care team looking after him now."

"That's good to hear." I smiled as I opened the cash drawer and started going through the dailies.

"Yes. I suppose," she looked around the little store, almost but not quite sneering as she did.

"Somebody is going to have to look after this for a few days. Until I can get some things finalized."

Without actually looking at me, she asks, "Would you mind? Though we could just shut it down, too."

Now she did look, agate eyes full of challenge.

"For Mr. B? I can look after it. Not a problem."

I say, my own eyes flinty hard, my chin up.

"Good. Now, might I have the key to the apartment please? There are a few things that he needs to make him more comfortable." Without a word, I handed over the little key ring that Mr. B. kept there. (He had a tendency to forget his actual set in the apartment in the mornings).

Carefully, she took the thing from my open palm and swished out the back door.

I finish the dailies, stash the cash, lock the door, and leave for home.

While I walk, I think about the look in Arabella's eyes when she asked me if I would look after the store. Did she think I was going to say "no", chicken out, and run like a rabbit? If that was the case, she obviously doesn't know me very well.

I figure she's one of those people who looks at someone and instantly judges them based on superficial bull-- like how they look. So, I'm not conventional. I have tats, my hair is a shaggy, multi-coloured mess that sticks out from my bandana like a leaf pile, I wear dark eye makeup, my fingernails are short, and the polish is chipped. My clothes aren't anything special, but they are comfy, and I wear runners or hiking boots. It's also fairly obvious that I don't belong to any organized religion.

Does that make me a bad person? No. It doesn't. As a matter of fact, I think of myself as a citizen of the Earth and a student of humanity. But when she sees "the packaging," does she immediately think the worst because I'm not perfectly coiffed and dressed in silks or whatever? I find it hard to believe that Mr. B. raised a daughter who was so shallow.

Or was she just a product of her current circumstances, fitting in because that is how her frenemies are?

It is a puzzle. And strangely, I can't get into her head to solve it, which is just as well because using my other senses that way without permission is an invasion of privacy. Technically. Though I have been known to – peek – occasionally. The next few days were comfortably routine. Everything was the same except that M. B wasn't there to greet me in the morning. And there was no sign of the number one daughter either. For which I thanked my Goddess regularly.

The fifth day, the day I expected Mr. B to return, well...

It starts out bad. I slept through my alarm. So, I have to slam down a piece of toast and a coffee—which is scalding hot and burns my tongue; throw on whatever clothes I can find that are clean (the nice thing about a wardrobe that's mostly t-shirts and cargo pants makes this a lot easier when you're in a hurry). But there isn't time to do much with the hair, so I slap on a ball cap and run out the door. No time for niceties, so I have to take the quick way to work.

There are places in any city that smart people avoid when they can. Sometimes it's the smell, most times it's the people who hang out there. But sometimes, it's a "feeling" that a place has. Even normal people have places they avoid, like the abandoned house at the edge of town that gives you the willies just thinking about it. Well, for sensitives, those places are the worst because we can hear the screams of the dying and the laughter of the twisted when we get too close. You get goose bumps; I get a million little fingers plucking at my clothes and hair. It's creepy as hell.

The roads I had to run down to take the shortcut were some of those places. I haven't been in this place long enough to know the history of these two streets. So, I have no idea what happened here or how long ago. But as I jog by the empty, broken windows and yawning doors, the sagging frames and weed-strewn yards, it takes all my concentration not to look left or right. It doesn't help that I'm the only idiot here either. That's breathing anyway. It's like the whole place has an interdiction on it to stop normals from living here. So, by the time I am clear of it and reach the bookstore, I'm red-faced, sweaty, and puffing like a blacksmith's bellows.

Arabella's fancy grey town car is there waiting for me.

Great. Just great! Could my morning possibly get worse?

Sighing, I hitch up my backpack and open the door. I hear the car door open and close and I am enveloped in a waft of Chanel No. 5, or whatever. I sneezed. Not in a ladylike way either. Blushing to the roots of my hair, I led the way inside. "Be wif u in a mom't. Need to find Kleenex." I garble out, ducking behind the counter. More or less all together again I stand up. Arabella is a little bit away, thumbing through a children's book. She is her usual elegant self. But her face seems troubled for some reason. A small frown puckers the skin between her eyebrows and her cherry red lips are pulled down at the corners.

I assume I was about to be browbeaten for being late. I tense up, ready for battle. Carefully, she returns the book to its place and turns to me. "Please tell me that you DO NOT live there!" she said in a tight voice. This is definitely not what I expected to hear. For a minute, I was flummoxed.

"No. On the other side, actually. But I slept in so I had to hurry....." I stammer.

"Well, Thank God you are that smart at least!" she ground out, relaxing a little. "I don't care how late it makes you, never do that again. I almost had apoplexy when I saw you run out of that street." She looks around. "Is there a coffee perk around here somewhere? I need a cup to settle my nerves."

"Uh. Yeah, in the storage room is a little table with coffee stuff on it..." I managed to say.

The rest of my brain has apparently checked out. If I didn't know better, I'd almost think she cared.

What the...?? Still confused, I got the store ready for the day. Arabelle returns, fresh steaming coffee in a cracked mug. Her jacket and scarf are gone, but everything else is the usual perfection. She drags an old stool from a corner and sits delicately.

"So. how has the store been doing while Papa is away?" she sips elegantly.

I hand her the stack of dailies. "Tonight, I run the z on the till. But sales have been decent."

"Mmm," she says as she thumbs through the paper slips.

"How is Mr. B. doing? I thought he'd be coming home today."

I'm trying to be casual about this. I doubt that I'm succeeding, though.

"Much better. He gets a little stronger every day. But I'm afraid that he won't be able to come back to the store. His health is too uncertain." Arabella looks at me, waiting for a reaction, I suppose.

"Damn that's too bad. He loves this place." I say, wondering what she wants me to say.

Or do. Oh, damn and blast! I'm gonna need a new job. She's gonna shut it down!

"Yes, he does," Her eyes travel around the room.

"You know it's funny. But this place hasn't changed much since we were children. The three of us would spend hours in that corner there doing our school work or whatever while Mama and Papa ran the store."

It was killing me because I was certain what the answer would be, but I had to ask, "So what happens now?"

Arabelle sets down her mug and looks me square in the face. I tense, ready for the blow. "It seems that Papa, even knowing he can't run it anymore, is unwilling to let the building go. I don't have the time to devote to it. Nor do my brother and sister. They have their own lives to live," she folds her hands.

"So, Papa and I were wondering if you would consider managing the place for a while. Until he changes his mind. You would receive an hourly wage, and, since he won't be needing it, you can move into the apartment upstairs."

Wow! Like wow! This was just too good to be true. Wait a minute...

"What's the catch?" I asked, hoping that my eyes weren't sparkling.

That would just be ridiculous. Actually, this whole conversation seemed ridiculously fantastic. There had to be a catch.

"You will be given a budget. You will act within that budget. All major changes must be cleared by Papa and I before they can happen. And you have to prove yourself a capable manager. If you do not, then you will be out on your ear."

"How much is the budget? What do you call major changes? What do you mean by capable?" I looked at her, already calculating things in my head.

"Name change for the store. B's Books is a tad outdated. We know it needs a new one. But we have to approve of the name you pick. Any structural changes to the outside of the building and living area have to be approved by us, and after that taken to the city for final approval. Basic repairs are to come out of budget. Major repairs as necessary to meet city code. By capable I mean that you have six months to start showing a profit. As it is at the moment, the building is barely making its bills and taxes. You are responsible for fixing that."

Arabella took a slip of paper and wrote an amount on it. "This is your budget for the next six months." she said, sliding it across the counter.

I think my eyes popped out of my head when I saw the numbers there.

"How much rent do I pay for the apartment? And what's my wage gonna be?"

Another paper. More numbers.

"Ok. You have a deal." I was shaking, inside, from absolute happiness. But, now that I'm a businesswoman, I didn't dare let it show. What I wanted to do was jump up and down like a little kid at the fair.

"Um. How does *Bell, Book and Candle* sound as a new name? I've always thought we needed to diversify to draw in more customers. You know, add regular and fancy candles, seasonal decorations, an updated style of book along with the classics....."

Tale 14: Interdiction

John and I watch from a safe vantage point inside the House as people come and go bringing all manner of things inside the building. John says that these are people who have been "moved" to help in response to the newspaper articles that were written about the House in the last little while. He assures me that things will settle down soon. After people have satisfied their need to "help". Personally, I can't wait. Not that I don't think it's nice that they are doing all this to aid the homeless and wounded people of this little corner of the world. I can appreciate that, even though I was never part of the largesse when I was alive (did that sound a little jealous? Oops). My biggest problem is the things they are thinking as they bring their goodies. Not all of them are being altruistic in their willingness to assist. And having all these people, well-intentioned or otherwise, coming and going seems more like a siege to me than anything.

Maybe I'm just being uber sensitive about it all after my little convo with Power numero uno. *I dunno*. Or maybe it's because my little sis is so busy she doesn't have time for me right now, and I'm not great with sharing. (Gimme a break. It wasn't all that long ago that I found out she is my sister. I'm still adjusting okay!). As I watch, I see a new person approach the steps to the building. She isn't carrying anything in, and it doesn't look like she's the type who might need to carry anything out. Her clothes are clean but well-worn. Her hair, which I suppose you might call honey blond, is pulled back in a neat ponytail. Nothing about her says needy, at least not in a physical way. Mentally, her thoughts are kind of a mess. She's got "a gazillion" projects on the go, and time seems to be a huge problem for her. *Curiosity piqued*, I excuse myself and sort of float down to get a better sense of who this person is and what she needs.

If I thought that outside the House looked like a building under siege, inside it looked like a beehive on steroids. There are people everywhere, and everybody is doing something. Myles looks like he is cataloging everything that is being brought in and taking particulars about the donors. A group of men is moving heavier stuff from the piles of goods into storage rooms on the main floor and down to the basement. Some of the women were sorting food into groups and stacking it neatly wherever they could find a spot. Others are sorting through clothing and laying it out according to size and type.

Wow! I knew (sort of) that a lot of stuff was being gifted to the House. But I had no clue that it was so much! If the whirring cameras were any judge, it would be a lot longer than John thinks before this settle down. News cameras were faithfully recording all the activity and all the noise generated by so many people jammed together in a building. It seemed that some of the volunteers had brought their kids with them too. Because the woman that I followed is busily trying to prevent a disaster as one of the youngsters and one of the guys carrying a chair would have collided if she hadn't had the presence of mind to grab the little twerp before it could happen. So naturally, since his mission was rudely interrupted by someone other than a parent, the kid in question immediately starts screaming blue murder! Come to think of it, even if it had been his mother, he was most likely gonna scream anyway...

And just like that, *EVERYTHING* stopped. All the noise (except for the boy exercising his lungs), all the adults quit rushing around, Myles quit furiously scribbling in his notepad, and *EVERYBODY* turned to look at the poor woman still holding the toddler. Blushing to the roots of her hair and beyond (hey fun fact that I just read the other day: did you know when you blush, so does the lining in your stomach? Isn't that way cool!), the woman sets the little snot ball down and he's immediately swept up by one of the women who has been organizing clothes. For a tense second or two I thought there was going to be some yelling and wild accusations flying around. But one of the camera guys saw the whole thing.

"She saved the kid from getting hurt. I have it on tape if you need to see," he said into the now total silence.

"He was going to run into the guy carrying the chair. The kid coulda have been hurt. For sure, the chair guy was."

The woman looks at the cameraman gratefully but stays silent. The mother and her little boy disappear into the crowd. Everyone else, except Myles and Chelsea, went back to whatever they were doing.

"*Hi,*" Myles says as he tries to juggle pens and paper so he can offer his hand to the woman.

"I'm Myles. And this is Chelsea." He drops a pen.

"Hi. I'm Mariposa. But most people just call me Mari." She shakes Myles' hand briefly.

"I'm sorry for causing a fuss. But he was right. The little boy was certain to get hurt. I acted without thinking."

"Oh, not a problem," Chelsea says as she watches Myles retrieve his ink stick.

"It's very busy here today. Nerves are stretched a little tight."

"I would imagine. What with everything that's been happening around here lately".

Mari smiles politely.

"So, what brings you to the House today? Did you bring something? Do you need something?"

Myles was unusually direct and looked a little harassed.

"No. Nothing like that. But thank you for the offer." Mari answers.

"Ok then. I'm gonna get back to work. Chelsea, I'll talk to you later."

Myles also disappeared in the crowd.

Would it be wrong for me to say he scurried away as fast as he could?

Why do guys do that when two women get together anyway?

I'm glad I never had to worry about the whole dating and boy's thing. So, I hung out with Chelsea and Mari for a bit, listening quietly as they chatted for a few minutes. It seems that Mari and her two young sons had managed to buy some old house in the area, and she was checking things out, get a sense of the whole area. Safe places to go. People willing to babysit. That sort of thing.

"Not that I will need anything like that right away. I've taken some time off to get the renovations at least started on the house. I gotta admit, though, I'm having issues finding contractors that have the time to do it." Mari sighs.

"Oh? That's a shame. Maybe I can help. There are a few people around here that are journey persons. I'll get a list together for you. You can pick it up in a day or so. We should have most of this stuff sorted out by then...." Chelsea says.

"Would you? Oh, that would be fantastic!! I've started peeling the old wallpaper off myself. But there are some things I'm just not brave enough to do. Like plumbing and electrical," she laughs.

"I totally get that. A few weeks ago, I had an issue with the bathroom tap in my apartment. Myles tried to fix it for me..the operative word there being tried. He's a lot of wonderful things. But he's no plumber." Chelsea giggles. And blushes a little. Awe! They are so cute!

"Well, I'll let you get back to it. Got a million things to do. Thanks for your help." Mari says as she makes her way through the people and ever-growing piles of stuff.

Interesting. But my innate curiosity still wasn't satisfied, so I decided to follow Mariposa for a little while. I want to know which house she's managed to buy that would be close enough to draw her to the House. I don't really need to, because honestly, it wasn't as though Mari could see me, but as she walked away from the House, I kept my distance while still keeping her in sight. Somewhere along the way, I have picked up D's habit of avoiding touching people as I walk by. Which, by the way, is no easy task when you realize how busy the street was at that moment. (More people heading to the House by the look of it; poor Myles.)

Everything is going well, I'm thinking that Mari's new home is closer than I expected, when she turns a corner that I am definitely not expecting her to take. My silent steps grind to a halt. She has just entered the area everybody around here refers to as No Man's Land: a block and a half of totally empty, dilapidated buildings that no sane person would live in. Or deliberately walk through. Even cops, if they are ever called to look for somebody in there, go in groups of three or more, and all of them are creeped out by the whole experience, according to Ramon anyway. Something about the whole area just screams wrong to everyone. Like a twelve-legged spider or a snake with two heads. Even addicts, pushers, and prostitutes give it a wide berth.

Sometime at the beginning of our relationship, John himself made me promise that I would never, under any circumstances, go down those streets. He never said why, and when I was just

Melody, I was too young to go that far from home, so it was never an issue. So, like everybody, I just avoided it, pretended it wasn't there, and got used to taking the long way around. I watched Mari walking down the street, seemingly totally unaware of the ambience of the place as she moved. No hurried steps. No unconscious rubbing of her arms. No furtive looking around. Absolutely nothing to suggest it was bothering her at all.

"Oh, this is bad. Very bad." I whispered as I flashed back to the House. I needed to talk to John.

***

I walk down the silent street, not really paying much attention, though, I do wonder why there aren't more people here. There are a lot of buildings here that are far gone into crumbling ruin. But there are still quite a few, like my own place, that could be so much more if they are given the time and attention they need. I guess there's no accounting for the vagaries of city life. Having brushed that aside, I start mentally making a list of all the things that I hoped to accomplish today and in the remaining two weeks of my "*vacation*" from work. It's a good thing that the boys are staying with their grandparents for a few more days. It makes it easier to work on the house if I'm not full-time parenting on top of everything else. Just thinking about all the work ahead of me was exhausting. But I'm nothing if not stubborn. But it really would be nice if Chelsea could get me a list of contractors that could help lift the weight off my shoulders.

Lost in my own thoughts it doesn't seem that long before I reach the end of the street and turn the corner and walk the last few yards to my home. Across the street, people are active again, doing their shopping and what not. I see the bookstore there and make a mental note to go in tomorrow. Maybe they will have some DIY books that will help speed things along.

Now where did I stuff the keys?

Somewhere in the bottom of my purse no doubt. Why does stuff like that always fall to the bottom and disappear? *Sigh*.

As I dig through the conglomerated disaster I call a purse, I can hear the moldy wallpaper in the living room calling out to me, daring me to pull it off and see what's underneath.

Good thing I'm stubborn. I think........

***

It's the end of the day, finally, and as I close and lock the door to Bell Book and Candle, I marvel at the good fortune that I never thought would ever happen for me. All made possible by a woman that was not as mean-spirited as I originally thought her to be.

Not that she's been easy on me either. Every change I want to make, she puts me through the loops and makes absolutely certain that I've done my research and due diligence before she tells me to go ahead, or not. All in all, though it seems to be working out. The books are showing a modest profit already, and I have a place that I can call my own for the very first time ever. Not bad for a kid from Nowheresville, which is around the corner from Nothing and Nobody.

Before I head up to my apartment though, I have to take a look around the corner of my street. Some of my customers were talking today about one of the old houses across the road. They say there are lights in the window. Gotta check it out for myself.

Who would be that stupid?

I step around the corner, and sure enough, there are lights on in one of the buildings. In the room that I assume is the living room, though with these buildings, you are never sure of the layout. Either way, the curtains or whatever are hanging all crooked, and the light shining through them makes them look like two yellow angry eyes staring balefully at the street. It gives me the shivers just looking at it. *Creepy old houses*!!

Obviously, whoever bought it has no idea. Maybe someday they might come into the store. Note to self: find a history book. Still creeped out I went home and ran myself a hot bath with cleansing herbs. I lit a few protection candles for extra insurance.

***

Myles and I both saw John and Melody waving frantically at us, but because of the crush of people in and out of the House, there wasn't anything we could do about it until the end of the day, when we were finally alone. John, of course, understood. Melody was beside herself and kept flitting in and out like a hummingbird. But now that everyone is gone, Myles and I are in the kitchen making a much-needed cup of tea to relax with while we listen to the major issue.

"Chels, you guys gotta do something! Like right now!" Melody insists as soon as she walks into the kitchen. "I have a very bad feeling. Something has to be done!"

Wow! I've never seen her so agitated and I know if we don't get her to calm down, we will never get to the bottom of the problem, whatever it is. "Melody. Breathe." I say to her, hoping it will help. Do Guardians even breathe? Certainly, her chest is rising and falling in her excitement and panic. But I'm pretty sure she isn't actually moving air.

Myles looks at John who just casually saunters in, the picture of calm efficiency. "John?"

"It appears that our new friend, I believe she said her name was Mariposa, has purchased a property at the edge of the dark street. Melody is concerned, and rightly so, that this is not a safe thing for her. Nor her children." John answers.

"Fortunately, it is on the edge of the troublesome area. But it is close enough to create potential problems."

"I see." Myles answers, most likely already thinking of possible solutions.

He sips the hot tea.

"If I remember from talking to her, the kids aren't with her just yet. She's there alone right now. But I seriously doubt that we can talk her out of moving. She seemed to really like that house. Was looking forward to fixing it up. Which reminds me, is there a list of local contractors that I can give her to help with the renos? Seems she's having trouble finding a contractor who has the time. I told her I'd ask you."

"NO! She can't stay there! Something awful is going to happen if she stays! She seems like such a nice lady. I want her to....." Melody interjects angrily.

"Melody!" John says, his usually soft voice hardened, probably more to get her attention than because he was angry. Melody catches the hint and shuts up.

"I understand your worry, child. I don't want anything to happen to her either. But she chose that house out of all the houses in the area that are for sale. Perhaps there is a reason that we aren't aware of yet. But if you continue to flit around like a confused bee, you may never see the reason and will have wasted time and effort for nothing." John soothes her.

"We will all keep an eye on our new friend in the coming days. We will do what we can to help when the need arises. In the meantime, there are others that we must look in on."

"Yes, John." Melody whispers, hanging her head a little.

A moment later and both the Guardians are gone. Myles and I both released a sigh of relief. For the moment at least there wasn't anything we could do. Which was good because we are both exhausted, and tomorrow promises to be as hectic as today. We need the down time.

Myles reaches out and wraps my fingers in his and squeezes gently.

"I'll get that list in the morning. Good tea," he says, watching me over the rim of his cup.

"Yes, it is nice," I answer, blushing from head to foot. When he looks at me like that, I can't help myself.

***

Things in my new house are finally starting to take shape. True to her word, Chelsea had the list of local journeymen who were willing to at least take a look at the project, ready the next time I stopped by the House of Enlightenment. Two had already come and gone, promising that they would have estimates for me in the next two days.

I have discovered, and can honestly say not surprised, that the walls beneath all that gross wallpaper are the old lath and plaster. Stained by mildew and neglect, they have to be removed and replaced by something more modern. And a decent layer of insulation was added. So, while I wait for the contractors, I work on a wall. It's amazing how satisfying it is to whack at the wall and pull stuff off. Rather cathartic, really. Anger, I didn't know I was holding inside, added energy to my swings, and the crunch and shoosh of stuff falling to the floor was emphasis and counterpoint to the thud and thwack.

I'm gonna hurt like crazy in the morning, using muscles I didn't even know I had. But at the moment.....

At first, in my mind's eye, I saw the face of my ex, whose disinterest and casual cruelty had finally convinced me that there was no point in continuing in a relationship that was contrived for the benefit of his parents and the world outside our doors. But gradually, thwack after thwack, his face morphed into the faces of the people around me now. At first, when I met them, they all seemed welcoming. Smiling, jovial, pleased that there is a new face in the neighborhood. But then I tell them where I am living, and it's like a shutter closing on a window. The window is still there, but I can no longer see it. Some have even taken a physical step back from me. Like, I have some kind of communicable disease they are afraid of.

It's confusing. It's painful. It's like Mark all over again.

Is there something wrong with me?

What will it be like when my boys get here?

How outcast will they be?

How deeply will the separation cut them?

I'm an adult, and it already hurts like hell, but I can ignore it. But they are just little boys. They don't have the defenses to handle the cruelty of strangers.

Thwack! Thwack! Thwack!

Mari, maybe this wasn't as good an idea as you thought. Thwack!

I can't feel them, but hot tears are making tracks in my dust-covered face.

I don't know how many hours (or minutes) I banged against that wall. But when I look behind me, there is a sizable pile of debris in the middle of the living room floor. Everything, including me, is caked in moldy plaster. The mess is incredible.

Insurmountable.

Indomitable.

Insuperable.

Unbeatable.

I collapse on my saggy, filthy sofa and cry myself into oblivion.

***

Even though, I am aware that John will disapprove, I make a special point of checking in with Mari at least once every day. Sometimes, twice if I can. Tonight, I blink in and the whole living room looks like a bomb went off in there. So, the first thing I do is check for gas leaks. (Neat trick that since I wasn't aware that I could actually smell until I consciously thought about it). There weren't any that I could detect. So now I go to the sofa and check on Mari herself.

Covered in plaster dust like everything else, a large mallet discarded on the floor beside her, she is curled up like a small child in the middle of her sofa. Obviously, she has been crying. Profusely, if the clean streaks are any way to judge.

So, what has she been crying about? Did something happen? Are her boys, okay?

There is no way to tell from the openly available evidence, though, I believe she was angry at some point during the destruction, and I'm reasonably certain she caused it. Again, though, why?

No choice then. I have to dig a little deeper. I kneel on the floor beside the sofa and gently lay my hand on Mari's brow. Surface thoughts are a jumble of emotions that I can't make any sense of, really. There is anger and sadness there. Loneliness. Exhaustion. And a whole range in between. I have to go a little deeper. Seek the reasons for it all. The pathways are twisty. Nothing is coming clear. It's all jumbled together like her emotions live in a blender permanently set on churn.

Cautiously, I worm my way through the maelstrom, trying to make sense of every image around me. It seems to take forever.

"Ray and Chelsea were easy compared to this," I mumble to myself.

Stubbornly, I keep going though. Each step was a blizzard of anger and despair, sadness and hopelessness. Then all at once, between one of her heartbeats and the next, I am through. And instantly terrified.

I find myself in a place of utter calm. No noise at all. No sounds of the body breathing, or the heart beating can be heard here. There is no light. It is utterly and completely black. A void. A pervasive nothingness. But I can sense that it isn't empty, either. So, with a little will, I make a small light. One that floats easily above my open palm. I do it as much to calm me, as a way to see where exactly I am.

Cautiously, I take a step, holding my little light in front of me.

At first, there is nothing but dark all around me and beneath me. Another step. Another. Another. There! At the edge of my light's reach, something curled up in a ball. Too big for a puppy. Not big enough for a sleeping dragon. *Another step*. The figure on the floor is Mariposa. Or I suppose her Id. Or her soul. Ok, whatever you want to call the inner construct of yourself. In any case, her.

But "*she*" isn't alone here. My skin prickles. *Another step*. Another. Looming over Mari's "body" is a figure. *Small, twisted*. A melted wax caricature where the face should be. The body is almost human and more terrifying for that, because in some way, it screams "wrong" to all my senses. The figure is leaning slightly over Mari. Protecting her? No. Something else. When I change my focus a little, I can see tendrils of some kind running from it to Mari and back again. Like a never-ending loop.

But the tendrils are thin. Imperfectly attached. New. And therefore, weak still. I hold my light a little higher, add a little more juice so it shines brighter. The wax face lifts.

The thing hisses, "*Go away. Mine.*" Its voice is raspy, reptilian, utterly inhuman.

"No. Not yours. Nor mine either. Her own." I say.

Add a little more juice. The light brightens enough that the thing slinks back a step.

"NO! MINE!" it hisses and tries to send out yet another streamer of whatever the hell that is. *Utterly, strangely, calm now*, I throw out the lighter and advance. "No. She isn't."

I toss my little ball of light upwards. It bursts against the surrounding dark, like a miniature sun. Just not as blindingly bright.

"Return to the dark that is your natural home. There is nothing for you here. Begone."

I say as I watch the anger and desperation bloom across the waxy face and into the eyes that are black as pitch. I roll my shoulders a bit, and from the sleeves of my coat, two long daggers slide into my hands, the metal hilts fitting comfortably there as I curl my fingers around them, solid, and oddly warm. I take the last step, and with a crossed slice, I sever the connection between Mari and her attacker. They snap back to the thing like taught rubber bands. It is visibly shaken by the pain that must have caused it. The anger and desperation turn to a towering rage. In seconds it has leaped over Mari's form and is attempting to attach its suckers to me.

Without thinking really, because there was no time to think, only react, I reached behind me and pulled a great sword from the hidden hilt under my jacket. I slash away the tendrils with the glittering blade, and they snap away, stinging their maker. It flows to my left, more tendrils. Dance around, turn, swing. Snap. Two more are gone.

Above me now. Raise the blade. Guard. Slash. Stab.

It retreats to eye level. Moves to my right and disappears in the gloom beyond my light.

I step over to Mari. But my eyes roam the darkness, knowing this fight is far from over. I close my eyes. Open my other senses. Listen and feel for any change that might give me a clue to where my adversary has gone.

Ah! There! Blade up and ready, I spin and meet the next attack.

It growls and hisses in anger and frustration and pain.

But I remain on guard. Each successive attempt to leech my life force(?) away met with steel and determination. Neither would I let it near Mari again. On we fought, it and I. Around and around in a great circle lit only by my little sun. And then, just like that, it was gone. It neither screeched nor threatened. It just left.

Which I find creepy as hell.

Mari moans slightly. I check her out. Everything looks okay.

I don't dare put the sword away, so one-armed, I help Mari rise. Slowly, we walked out, my light ball much diminished but dancing (I mean that literally, because the thing was bobbing along like it was drunk) slightly ahead of us. We passed through the emotional blender zone, much slower now, so I could see/read what the problems were, then deposit Mari in a happy dream of her childhood. There was no more sign of whatever that was, so I put away the sword.

And utterly spent and weirded out, I went back to the House. Not exactly sure what had just happened. Not sure what the consequences were likely to be either. And right at this moment, too tired to care, even though I know I'll have to tell John.

***

A couple of days go by before I see anybody that I could talk to about the happening in Mari's head.

"And from nowhere you are suddenly carrying weapons? Like daggers and swords? Seriously?

Wow!" says Chelsea after I told the whole story.

"Where are they now?" John asks, blue eyes thoughtful, fluffy eyebrows puckered in concentration.

"I have no idea. I looked for them after I got back. But they were gone. And I know for certain they weren't there earlier." I insisted.

This is beginning to feel more like an interrogation than anything.

"Honest. Heck I even tried calling them forth. But I got nothing."

"Hmmm." John says.

"How is Mari?" Chelsea asks. "I assume you've dropped in at least once since then?"

"She seems okay. Not getting any strange thoughts from her. No sign of her interloper either. But I don't know her well enough to say she's totally unscarred by any of this."

"Gonna have to keep an eye on her for a while," Myles says, looking sideways at John, who nods without answering.

"Alright, Captain Sparrow, if you're all done swashbuckling for the rest of the week, I'm tired and would like to get some sleep. So, if you don't mind, I'm going to say g'night." Chelsea puts her cup in the sink and heads for the door.

It wasn't until after she left that even thought to ask who Captain Sparrow was anyway....

Tale 15: W.A.S.

Warriors Angels Survivors

As I watch Myles talking with a group in the foyer, I realize it's time. Time to call the number of the therapist that my social worker had given me months ago. After I had been attacked. So far, he has been very patient with me. Not pushing or pressuring me at all to take our relationship to the next level. But I know he wants to. It's there in the warmth of his eyes, the crooked smile, the little touches every time he gets close. Mostly so do I ; because those same looks and smiles and touches make my heart beat harder, make my skin tingle and the sun shines brighter whenever he's around.

But I'm horribly afraid. Afraid that he will be disappointed and leave. Afraid that I will be forever tainted by the mental wounds that I have yet to deal with. Afraid that I will freeze up. Or chicken out at the last minute because my body remembers the pain and degradation of the attack, even though my waking mind does not.

And if I do freeze up, what then?

How do I handle it?

How will he?

Will it take something special and turn it into a disaster?

And hurt us both beyond fixing?

Yes. Time to recover my Self. For my own sake. And his. It's taken the better part of two weeks, but the huge influx of well-wishers and do-gooders has finally slowed to a trickle. So, I'm okay to escape for a couple of hours. But first, I have to make the call. Too many people out here to have any expectation of privacy, so I can't use my cell; too many people coming and going in the kitchen as well. So that leaves the office where Myles spends most of his time on normal days.

The group with Myles breaks up so I use the opportunity to approach, "Myles. I need to make a call. Would you mind if I used the office? I'll only be a few minutes."

"Sure, not a problem. Is everything all right? Never mind, that's none of my business. Sorry." he lowers his head apologetically.

"I have to double check the count in storage room two anyway. If I'm not back in twenty minutes, send in coffee and a couple of Rose's doughnuts." he quips.

Storage room two is where we put all the yoga mats and blankets that have been donated. "That done, are you?" I say, squeezing his hand.

"Girl, you got no idea," he sighs dramatically. He looks around. Spies, another group that seems to be making a beeline towards us. "Gotta go." he says, walking away as decently quick as possible without looking like he's running. I smirk and head in the opposite direction.

As I suspected, the therapist couldn't see me immediately, but we made arrangements for an initial meeting in a couple of days. She sounds nice on the phone. Young, but not too young, which I think is good. I doubt that I could talk to somebody too close to my age or old enough to be my grandmother about any of this. I'm not really good with opening up to strangers at all.

Gee, I wonder why?

The therapist's office was a short bus ride away. I could easily have walked the distance, but it was unseasonably warm today, and I didn't want to arrive all sweaty and hot.

The building is a small office structure three storeys high. In the movies, it would likely be described as non-descript and ordinary. No big flashy signs to tell you who and what may be inside. Just a list of placards with neat, simple names.

CANDO Therapies is on the second floor.

The elevator whizzed me up in no time. With a swish, the doors open onto a lobby with a single desk and a few upholstered chairs. There is artwork and plants, a fish tank and soft music (a Brahms Waltz, I think) playing in the background. The woman at the desk looks up and smiles as I approach.

"Good afternoon." she says.

"Um. Hi. I'm here to see Candace?" my voice seems a little shaky suddenly.

My spit has dried up too.

"Okay. I'll let her know you're here. In the meantime, much as I hate to, I need you to fill out these forms."

She hands me a clip board with a couple of questionnaires and a pen. I notice immediately that the chairs are super comfy as I sit with my papers. All the standard questions are there. It only takes a few minutes and I'm done. I hand the board back. To Sheila, according to her name tag.

"Perfect!" she says as she takes them. "Couple more minutes, and she'll be right with you."

Generally, *"couple more minutes"* is code for it's going to be at least thirty before you get in, so I consign myself to a long wait and pick up a magazine. It occurs to me that it's odd there isn't anyone else in the waiting room. Or signs of any person at all except Sheila and myself. Sheila is humming along with the music now as she types away on her laptop. Maybe five minutes later, true to Sheila's word, a woman steps out into the short hallway.

About the same height as me, dressed in loose slacks and a simple t-shirt, canvas sneakers on her feet, a smile that lights up her dark eyes, dark hair cut in an angular pixie that frames rather than hides her face. Soft touches of makeup. It is impossible to guess her age. But there is strength and confidence in her bearing that puts me at ease. I relax a little more.

"Hi Chelsea. I'm Candace."

She takes the last step and offers her hand. I rise and accept the handshake.

"Come on back and we'll chat." She walks beside me and opens the door.

Having never been to a therapist before, and only having old tv shows and movies to go by, I expected to see a large desk and a long-padded couch and certificates on the walls. Maybe a few art pieces and a plant (for atmosphere). What I stepped into could have been somebody's kitchen. A round wooden table dominates the space, with a spray of fresh flowers in the centre. Soft, padded chairs sit around the table. The single large window has curtains in a tiny floral pattern, smooth and without frills. Light from the window enters the space and makes lighting unnecessary, though I saw that there were a few lamps in the corners. One wall was taken up by cupboards and counter space. Uncluttered except for a coffee maker and a tea kettle, sugar in a crystal bowl and creamers. And a small microwave.

"Not quite what you expected, huh?" she says as she watches my reaction.

"No. Not really." I say.

"People who see me for the first time are always surprised. They expect this to be like a visit to the doctor, you know, all clinical and stiff. But I find they open up more in a space that is less intimidating. Something more like home. The ultimate goal is to let you know you can trust me, like a favorite aunt, and you can talk to me about anything, and I won't judge. It doesn't work for everybody of course. So, there's another, more traditional office across the hall. My partner uses that one often. Most of his clients are men. I see mostly women. Who seems to be more comfortable chatting in the kitchen over coffee and cookies? Speaking of which, have a seat. Can I get you anything? Coffee, tea, chicken soup?"

I laugh. "You would actually make me chicken soup?" I say as I select a chair facing the counter.

"Heck ya. Chicken in a mug and crackers in the cupboard. Comes in handy in the winter. So, coffee?"

"Yes, please."

A moment or two later, Candace and I are comfortably seated at the table sipping hot fragrant coffee, a plate of chocolate chip cookies on the table beside us.

"So. What's up kiddo?" she asks, looking at me over the rim of her cup.

Where do I begin? I know already that even without thinking about it, I'm going to tell this woman everything.

***

Of course, I have heard about the House of Enlightenment/St Therese's through all the media coverage it has received of late. I have thought about checking it out for myself. But I haven't taken the time. Now, after listening to Chelsea tell the back half of her story (I want to hear it all, but I have other clients so it will have to come in increments of an hour at a time), my interest is growing. At the moment she makes her fella sound like a paragon of virtue. Not surprising, she obviously loves the guy. It seems that the feeling is mutual. I'm impressed that he isn't the pushy type. Will have to investigate further. Chelsea herself is an empathetic young woman, well suited to looking after other people. But like all such, she has a tendency to pass over her own needs in favor of theirs and therefore doesn't deal with her own issues. Having her come to see me is a huge step for her. She is aware that her inner life is off kilter and is wise enough, despite her youth, to know that she needs help in order to deal with it. The trauma of the rape (I suspect) is only the most recent in a long list of things that have happened to that girl in her life. Slowly, together, we will bring them out into the light.

It will take time, however, to undo the damage that has been done. For now, we will concentrate on her inner feelings and fears about sex and abandonment. See where it leads from there. She would be a good candidate for the *W.A.S.* Meetings when they start. I mentioned it. She has said that she will set out some flyers for me at the House and around her neighbourhood. Perhaps this will be better than I had hoped. Chelsea has promised to return in three days for another meeting. I believe she is committed to her own well-being at this point, so I see no reason to believe otherwise.

***

Chelsea has indeed returned for a second meeting with me. As before we met at the table. She is more relaxed and willing to talk today than in the first meeting. It appears that she passed out from the beating that took place along with the rape so there are no true memories of the event. I took her through a cognitive interview and gleaned as much information as possible that way. If there were any words spoken by the rapist, even under cognitive interview she does not recall them. I asked her to describe the injuries her body suffered as a result.

I have seen the medical reports on file for the incident. She knows about most of them because of the resultant scarring. She has a tendency to gloss over the worst ones, however. Possibly an unconscious avoidance behaviour.

More work will be required there. I believe these to be the core of her fears. Muscle memory can recall the trauma perhaps. She is still not wholly comfortable with the idea of intimacy with her boyfriend. He apparently shows incredible patience in this regard. Chelsea herself is more driven to succeed believing that lovemaking with Myles will erase the memory of the rape. When asked if she ever dreams about it, she reports that at this point, she does not remember her dreams, but has woken occasionally in the middle of the night, breathing heavily, with her blankets and sheets twisted. I have asked her to keep a journal beside the bed so that when she is awoken, she can write down anything she does recall, even if it is only one word.

N.B. Chelsea still refers to the rape as "*the attack*". To date, the perpetrator remains at large.

On a side note, as promised she has distributed the flyers and has promised to attend the meeting. Time to get my own ducks in a row and set up the venue with chairs and such. Still have not made the time to visit St. Therese's as yet. Chelsea is slated for another meeting next week.

***

Twice now I've been to see Candace at her office. It is indeed like having coffee and cookies with an aunt.

Gee I wonder if I do have an aunt or an uncle in some place?

Wouldn't that be cool?

Wonder what Melody would think of the idea of having a larger family than just us?

And John and all the others here at the House.

Candace says she wants to stop by some time and see what all we do here. I told her she is welcome any time. I suppose that means that I should tell Myles that I'm seeing a therapist, so that I don't have to fib to him about it. I hope he isn't disappointed in me. Honestly, I'm getting a little tired of talking so much about the attack. There has to be more to me than just that one thing. But then on the other hand, if I'm not ready to move it up with Myles, I guess I'm not done really dealing with it either.

I wonder what the *W.A.S.* Meeting is going to be like? I hope lots of people come. I have flyers sitting in the foyer of the House, and I've seen them taped to windows at Bell Book and Candle and KG's market. Ramon and Georgiana have taken a few as well to distribute wherever they can. So that's good.

Wow! Is that the time?

I better stop daydreaming and get busy. These sandwiches aren't going to make themselves. Why is it when my mind is super busy my hands seem to stop moving?

I'm weird.

Myles is coming. I can smell his aftershave even from here. Sweet but spicy. Earthy but not heavy. Whatever it is, I like it. It suits him. Sometimes, I can't wait to have that smell all over me. *Hopefully soon.*

***

The day of the first *W.A.S.* Meeting is finally here.

I'm a therapist damn it, but I'm unaccountably nervous. In fact I'm presently hiding out in the bathroom contemplating throwing up my lunch.

How sad is that?

What if nobody showed up?

What if they do show up but hate me?

I look at my reflection in the mirror. I tell myself, "Get a grip," and head out to the little hall I rented for this occasion. I take one deep breath and open the door. I paste a smile on my face, look neither right nor left, and walk to the front where the lectern awaits. I look out at the sea of faces; women, men, children even. Some still showing the outward physical signs of what they have gone through, may still be going through. Others cower in their chairs trying to be as inconspicuous as possible, terrified they will be recognized maybe. Or just plain terrified. Still others sit cross-armed, looking belligerent and nasty pretending to a toughness they don't really feel. But they are all here. And that's a start.

My heart breaks for each and every one of them. A long, hard road lies ahead for each and every one. Some will survive, mostly intact. Some will shatter like glass. Some will not be here for the next meeting.

Which is the point of this gathering?

To improve the odds for as many as possible. The thought gives my wobbly legs strength, stops my heart from hammering its way out of my chest, adds extra warmth and truth to the welcoming smile that I send out to them.

I am here for them. And for me.

"Welcome, everyone to our first meeting. My name is Candace. I will be your convener for the evening. I know some of you are scared and nervous about being here. You're afraid that you will have to come up and tell everyone why you are here. Those of you that want to, are certainly encouraged to do so if you would like. But ONLY if you want to. It isn't a prerequisite for being here. This is a safe place. A place that I hope will show you that you are NOT alone. As a group we are here for each other. Because we ALL understand how you feel. We know your pain and your fear as intimately and intensely as you do. We've been there. We are there. We swim in a sea of humanity. And like all seas, there are sharks in the water. Some you can tell immediately are best to be avoided. But some come really well disguised as Mothers, Fathers, Uncles, Neighbours, Husbands, Friends, Bosses, Doctors, Policemen, Priests."

"I know how scary that is. Because really, who can you trust?

Especially for those of us that seem to have a big red "X" that means Pick Me because we've already been there.

We'll talk about that in a moment.

First, though, is the question of trust.

One way or another, through sexual abuse, physical abuse, or mental abuse, trust has been beaten out of you. So, you live in fear of everybody. You might be really good at hiding it, but it's there.

You might be spending all your time trying to make everybody else happy. But it's there. Affecting how you look at the world.

How do you look at yourself?

Once you've lost trust, it's incredibly hard to find it again. Even here inside your head and your heart.. In fact you may never trust everybody again. Except maybe a very few people that you let yourself get close to. And that's okay. It's what you need to do to be a survivor in this shit storm that life has given you. I'm hoping, eventually, you will at least learn to trust this group a little and believe the things we are trying to teach you here.

One of the things we hope to teach you is that the big red "X" you carry is a beacon that the sharks of this world use to hone in on you. It's there in the way you walk, talk, sit, act, and think about yourself. But it isn't your fault. Early in life, something put it there. So, if you want to get rid of that mark, trust yourself. You have very refined and learned instincts when it comes to other people. *Listen to that little voice.*

Become the Warrior brave enough to realize you are worth loving, worthy of living. That what has happened to you in the past isn't right, isn't fair, and *ISN'T YOUR FAULT*. A warrior brave enough to walk away from the horrid nightmare situation. Brave enough to tell somebody about the bad thing that happened or is happening, and keep telling until it is finally stopped.

Not so long ago, abuse of any kind was a dirty secret that nobody talked about but everyone knew about. Something that police and doctors, and social workers had no idea how to deal with. But it isn't a secret anymore. Whole departments are set up for us so we can safely come and tell our stories and be *believed*. There is special training courses set up that they have to take before they can work in those areas.

There are people out there who care. You need to find your inner *Warrior*, your inner *Angel,* and *Survive*.

You need to do this because there have been too many of us who didn't have time, or didn't have enough strength left to find their inner Warrior. They became angels instead. Some of you may already know a person or persons who are no longer among us.

These are the reasons I've named this group, this gathering *W.A.S.*

"W" for the warriors you are, because you came tonight.

"A" for the angels who were not so lucky.

"S" for Survivor, because no matter what, we did it.

We survived.

For one more reason as well that just occurred to me: What was does not ever need to be again. The Past was. The Present is. The Future will be whatever you decide to make it. Thank you for listening to me. If you have any questions, I'll be over there with the coffee and cookies."

I sip gratefully at the scalding hot coffee. Now in the aftermath, my fingers shake a little as I hold the paper cup. I breathe. I wait to see if anyone will come talk to me. It will be my first small sign that I have managed to reach at least some of these people. I see Chelsea weaving her way through the little knots of people. I am so glad to see a familiar, friendly face

"Wow. Good talk," she says, getting her own drink. Her hands aren't shaking.

"Thanks. Do you think it worked?" I wonder aloud.

She shrugs noncommittally. "Tell me more about the big red X," she asks.

"Every person you know unconsciously telegraphs how they think of themselves in the way they behave. Especially people who are or have been abused. They present to everyone else as fearful, afraid, and ashamed. They give off little unconscious clues. Other people are very good at reading those clues, and they can take advantage of an individual that they see as weak."

And now I have an audience again.

Chelsea seems not to notice, though. "So, are you saying that I brought on my own rape, because I was sexually abused as a little kid?" her eyebrows pucker.

"In your case, I think it was probably more a matter of bad timing. Though you may have been. I didn't know you then, so I have no way of saying for certain. It seems to be more prevalent in people who have suffered significant abuse over time."

"So more than just the once, then." Chelsea sighs in obvious relief.

Another woman steps to the front of the gathering crowd around Chelsea and I. Her manner is belligerent, angry, and frustrated.

"I think the name of this group shoulda beed *If I Only Had a BAT*."

"I understand your feeling of anger. I know you would like to get revenge on your abuser. It's a very real and normal reaction in situations like the ones you have all been through. I get it. I really do." Around us, there are murmurs of agreement and snickers and snorts and other less kind noises.

"Except that violence only self-perpetuates. He is violent to you. You are violent back. And the problem only escalates instead of being fixed. And then you're both in Jail, and Junior learns that violence is normal for a home. So, his own home becomes violent, and the cycle continues. I want to break the cycle. Before it goes any further. So as enticing as it might be to take a bat to hubby's melon, in the long run, it isn't going to get you very far. And ultimately solves nothing."

There were murmurs of agreement and disagreement. But it was a start. Now the conversation could truly begin. But it was going to be a long two hours, which is how long I've rented the hall for. It wasn't until later, at home in my own bed with Fester my cat curled up beside me that I realized that Chelsea had finally called it rape. *Good for her*. She was coming out the other side.

Tale 16: Not Everything is a Success Story

I stand on the corner across from the great stone building and watch the comings and goings there. The late summer sunshine is warm and reflected back to me from the pavement and the stones. I should be hot standing here. Or at least, very comfortable. But my wasted body is cold. I don't believe I will ever be warm again. Haven't been warm for a very long time.

Why did I come back?

There is nothing for me here but pain-filled memories. *Memories.* Existing, half wild and filthy, on the back streets only a few blocks from here. Being rescued, so to speak, by the very building I now stare at, looming over me, savior and accuser both. Becoming "*real*" again instead of just a shadow among shadows. Job after job, not competent at any of them. The weight of failure is pushing down on me more and more each day. The only bright moment was the birth of my daughter, *Melody*.

But even that was torn away from me. They said I was so brave at her funeral. In fact, I was numb. Cold. I sat alone, because I was alone. In my heart was nothing. Except anger, maybe. But even that was not enough. I have never been enough. My choices have never been completely right. I never completely drug myself out of the cesspool that my life was then and still is. Hooking was a means to an end. It paid the bills and, more importantly, paid for the habit those stupid doctors gave me after the stabbing. It took away the pain then and it made me forget how shitty everything was later. By the time Aria was born, though I tried, it was too late. The hooker was hooked, a wriggling fish on a line controlled by my pusher/pimp.

For years that feel like centuries. I heard he died. Shot by a cop. Of course, by then, I was in jail or an institution or whatever you want to call it. Aria is long gone. Hopefully safe and happy. I had thought about looking for her after I got out, but I took the coward's way and didn't. *Better for her. Better for me.*

Moved right the hell out of this forsaken hole as soon as I could. Tried to make something out of the nothing. Maybe I succeeded in a small way. Of course, none of that matters now anyway.

The papers made a big deal about "*The House of Enlightenment*" after that whole thing with the deacon's brother killing everybody. Maybe that's why I'm back here. One last look. Maybe. *I dunno*. Or maybe I'm looking for one last rescue.

****

The teenager didn't see the scrawny old lady standing on the corner, half in, half out of the shadows. He barreled around the corner, laughing as he sprinted ahead of his friends, youth and exuberance and energy fueling his muscles and driving him on. Five seconds later, the old lady was lying barely conscious on the sidewalk and his friends were all staring in shock, saying, "Man! What did you do?" in breathy whispers. The unlucky young man, unable to move away or move forward, could only mouth "Oh my god, oh my god, oh my god, oh my god!"

Luckily, there were enough pedestrians in the area who were quicker thinkers than the young men. One of them had some training in first aid.

"Ma'am? Can you hear me?" he asked even as he carefully looked for injuries and watched the rise and fall of the bony chest.

She stirred a little in response, but didn't open her eyes.

"Ma'am? Where are you hurt?"

She moans in response.

"Somebody needs to call 911. And I need a blanket or a coat or something to cover her with," he demands of the various onlookers.

The prospect of a hospital trip apparently dragged the woman out of limbo. "No. Damn. Hospitals," she whispers.

"Well, at least let the ambulance guys give you a once-over. Once they get here."

"Not hurt. Just had my eggs scrambled." For a moment, she struggled to sit up on her own. For one reason or another, she was unable to, so, grudgingly, she asked for assistance.

"Help me sit up, would you? Please."

By now of course a small crowd had gathered around the accident, which drew the attention of people elsewhere on the street, not least of which were Chelsea and Myles, who were both currently in the House office organizing times for their various groups and gatherings.

"Wonder what that's all about." he said softly when he noticed the gathering throng of pedestrians.

A second later his question was answered when a slight shift allowed him to see a person lying on the sidewalk being covered by somebody's jacket.

"Looks like somebody got hurt," Chelsea said, as she grabbed a small cushion from a nearby chair and made long strides for the front door.

Myles followed close behind, pausing long enough to grab a small first aid kit he kept in the bottom drawer of the desk. A moment later, they had joined the crowd. Most of which were doing nothing so much as taking up space and taking videos with their phones. Carefully they made their way through to the man and woman at the center.

"Ma'am. I don't think that's a good idea. Maybe you'd be best to just lie still until the ambulance gets here," the unknown rescuer replied as he pressed gently on her shoulders to stop her from moving.

"Hi. Is there anything I can do to help?" Myles asked as he joined the pair on the sidewalk. "I have a kit if we need it," he added as he laid it down and snapped open the latches.

"911's been called. I think," he looked up at the bystanders expectantly.

"But the lady doesn't want to go to the hospital. I couldn't see any visible wounds or bleeding. She seems to be breathing fine. But that doesn't mean much at her age." he answered.

"Why is it rescuers and doctors all talk about a person when they're right beside them as though they have suddenly been struck deaf and senseless?" the woman grumped.

"I'm right here and I can hear you, you know!"

Chelsea knelt down by the woman's head. Gently, she stroked the thin layer of hair, soothing the woman while checking for lumps and other malformations of the head.

"I brought a pillow for under your head. Would you like it?" she offered gently after she was satisfied there were no obvious depressed fractures.

"Does anything hurt or feel tingly? Don't worry. It will be okay..."

"Don't worry. It will be okay...." For a moment the soft touch, the soft voice took me back in time.

To a place where I was loved. Aria holding me, just like this, stroking my hair... My eyes burned with sudden tears. I felt a couple of falls before I could blink them away. But I opened them fully now and looked at her. The same eyes I remembered. Soft brown. But there was a hint of sadness and bitter truths there as well. The same face, without the baby softness. The same little half smile. I reached up to touch this apparition from a long but never forgotten past and fainted dead away.

"I think she just fainted, Myles," Chelsea said, looking at the two men kneeling there with her as she held the hand that so briefly touched her face.

"Well, that might be a good thing. At least there won't be any more arguments about going to the hospital..." Myles replied.

They could hear the sirens now as the ambulance driver used them to pass through a red light. A few moments later, it pulled up to the curb. The crowd parted to let them through. They gathered the information that they could, gently loaded the casualty on the gurney and sped away. And everyone else went back to business as usual with a little story to tell their friends and family and coworkers.

**

"The flibbertigibbet is flying into the fuferall," Myles said, slightly exasperated.

"Mmm. Is it?" Chelsea answered as she hugged the small pillow to her chest and gazed out the window, unseeing the world outside.

"OK, Chels. What is it? For the past hour, all I've gotten from you is nonsense. You obviously haven't been listening. What's up? And don't say nothing. You haven't really been here since we got back from the accident across the street." With gentle fingers, he turns her head and makes her look at him. "Is it something about that lady? Do you want to go see her?"

"Oh, Myles, I'm so sorry. I wish I could explain. There was something. But I don't know what. I can't explain it. It's just something..familiar. But not. I don't know. Maybe I should go. Try and make sense of this, whatever it is."

"OK. Grab your saddlebag and we'll go."

"You don't have to….." Chelsea started to say, then changed her mind when he gave her that look that generally meant "don't argue".

**

"Hi. There was an older lady brought in by ambulance a while ago. She fell on the sidewalk and hit her head. I was wondering if I might see her?" Chelsea explained to the woman behind the counter.

"Are you family of hers?" the receptionist asks.

"Well, no. But we were there when it happened. I don't know if she even has a family."

"Rules say I can't help you then. Only information is given to family, family services or the police. Sorry."

"Well, nuts!" Chelsea said as she stepped away from the desk.

"Now what do we do?" Chelsea gazed around her at the sea of people. Some doctors or nurses. Some police persons. Some in suits. But most are in pain of one sort or another.

"I could never work in a place like this." she said. "So, much misery in one place."

"I know what you mean," Myles answered, rubbing Chelsea's arm.

He was looking around, hoping to find a familiar face that might be able to get them where they wanted to go. No such luck. No Ramon. No social worker. No, John or Melody, either for that matter.

"Come on," he said, leading Chelsea slowly and carefully through the scattered chairs and personal belongings.

"Maybe we'll get lucky and see her. Or hear her…"

"Or maybe some overworked nurse will point us in the right direction," Chelsea added.

**

I watched Myles and Chelsea begin their wander through the sea of people in the hospital, wanting to help by directing them to the little cubicle at the back where she was laying, half asleep, remembering. In a strange way it hurt me that I could not help them any more than I could help her. I thought I had at the time when she first came to my church. The ladies and I had done everything that we knew how to do to get her on the right track, make her healthy again.

In my hubris, I was certain it had worked. Sure, that she was leaving us healed and whole. But, sadly, the wounds that we could not see could not heal. Broken, she came to us. Broken, she left us. Now I stand watch over her, as I could not and did not in life. And I wait.

Too little, too late. One of my few regrets.

*** **

It wasn't something that I could put my proverbial finger on, but I could tell that there was something up with John. He seemed sad this morning when I saw him. And now he was conspicuously absent even though there were things and people that we had planned to visit today. Come to think of it, I hadn't seen Chelsea or Myles for most of the afternoon either.

Where the heck did everybody go?

*****

Chelsea and Myles, after 30 minutes of wandering, decided to stop at the nearest kiosk for a drink to consider their options. They had been unsuccessful at that point in locating the lady on their own, and the professionals they asked were less than helpful. It was beyond frustrating.

"We have to find her soon." Chelsea said quietly between sips of bottled water.

"I can't explain it. But we need to find her." There was determination and urgency both within that statement.

"Time to bring out the big guns then," Myles stated with a half-smile.

For a second, Chelsea looked at him like he'd lost his mind. Then he winked, and she knew what he was referring to. It wasn't strictly necessary, but for some reason, she felt the need to hold his hand while they "*called*" for help. A moment later, Melody, bright and effervescent as always, stood before them. John had not answered.

"Hey guys. What's up? Have you seen John? I haven't seen him in a while." casually, Melody stepped sideways to avoid touching (or being touched by) a person on his way to wherever.

Under the pretense of talking to each other, they explained the situation to Melody.

"Ok. So, we're looking for some nameless elderly person that you desperately need to see. In a hospital half full of elderly, nameless people who need someone to see them. I think they call that irony. Wait here. I'll see what I can do."

*****

I heard Myles call out to me. I know Melody answered. So, she was in the building now too. The wait wouldn't be much longer. To facilitate things, I came out of hiding so that I at least could be a beacon for the child now careening through the various rooms disrupting others as they tried to do their work. *So much to learn….*

*** **

The instant that John turned himself back "on", I felt it and after that finding him (and the lady) was easy, if a little perplexing. Why would he be standing guard over some nameless woman? Time enough to solve that mystery later.

"Follow me." I said to Chelsea and Myles and led them to the woman's cot side.

John stepped back from his place so that Melody could take his place at the woman's right hand. Chelsea moved to her left. Myles remained at the foot of the bed. In that moment, the woman, whose name had once been Helena, then Kip, opened her eyes from the half dream to look at the people by her side.

"I thought you were a dream. But here you are. I didn't think I would ever see either of you again. There are so many things that I want to say. To both of you. But I suppose the most important thing is that I'm sorry. That I wasn't a better mother. Or, a better person. Or, made better choices."

Salty tears leaked from the corners of the rheumy eyes.

"I tried sometimes. But it never worked out the way I wanted. I always screw it up in the end. But I need you to know that I never, ever regretted having you two. You were the brightest and best thing that I ever did. I'm sorry that I never got to see either one of you grow up. But, look what fine beautiful women you turned out to be."

"It's okay, Mama. We understand."

Chelsea answers, using the sleeve of her shirt to wipe away the dampness on Helena's face. Very carefully. Half in and half out of the world as she was, there was no telling what Helena would be able to read from skin-to-skin contact. She didn't need to know about the things Chelsea had survived. It would only cause her more pain. This moment was more about comforting than condemning. But it would be so easy….. Melody of course dared not touch her at all. But Chelsea, Myles and John could read all of the emotions roiling under the surface of her mobile face.

"Do you know why I named you Melody and Aria? Because music has always seemed like a beautiful thing to me. Even in my darkest moments, if there was music, I could find my way out again. You were my music. My light in the dark."

Moments later, Helena was asleep again. After Myles led Chelsea away, Melody and John stood alone by the bedside. Helena was sleeping. Not quite comatose. But more deeply asleep than was normal.

"So that's what became of our mother," she sighs sadly.

"Had I done my job better, perhaps it might have been different. For both of you. You would still be alive, and Chelsea's life may not have mirrored so closely the life of her mother. Possibility and probability juxtaposed."

"Is that what you've been beating yourself up about all day? What would you be saying to Myles right now if it were him? To be human is to be fallible. Mistakes happen. Intended or not. The important thing is that you tried your best."

Melody looks at the frail figure on the bed.

"The same could be said to her. But there's nothing I can do about that now," she sighs, heavily.

A dark figure weaves its way through the many beds in the room, heading, obviously to Helena's. It is not, however, D, but one of the others who comes to take care of business.

"Nuh uh, Buster. This is my mother, and the only one who's gonna take her to whatever, is Desmond. And I will wait right here until he can come. I don't care if it takes a week."

"She might care squirt." Is the rumbling reply.

But before Melody could put together an answer, a softer more familiar voice says, "Hey kid. I heard you might need me."

Tale 17: Happy Endings

Everybody should have a happy ending to their story. But in my line of work, and in the place that I work, happy endings are few and far between. Endings are often messy, tearful affairs usually involving blood and various other forms of gore. *It's sad, really.* The things that people do to other people. Sometimes for no decent reason.

I try, usually, to finish the job as politely as possible given the circumstances. But then, there is no accounting for people and what they think they deserve versus what they end up with. Some fight tooth and nail for each gasping breath, sure they were meant to die rich, famous, happy. Or they think they should still have a bunch of years left, and I showed up way too early. The easiest ones by far are the ones who have already been given a terminal diagnosis and have had time to prepare for the inevitable. They are at least glad that it will be over finally.

A very few see me arrive, know it is their turn, and surrender easily if not happily. Most of these have lived a good, long life, accomplished most of their goals. They are mostly pleased with the way things they had a hand in turned out. So, there is no angst or anger. *Just acceptance.* The ones that bother me the most (other than babies and little kids) are the fourteen to twenty-somethings that will never grow up, or feel all those firsts that are supposed to be so special for each person.

Their parents will stand by the graveside and wonder, "Why," as they cry a river of salty tears. But there is never an answer. Not from anybody. Not from the Powers that Be, or the entities, like me, who work for them. *It isn't fair.* But that's the way it is. *Sucks.*

Not that there isn't, or can't be, happiness in the world. I guess you just need to know where to find it. When I need a lift (yes, even Death needs a pick me up occasionally), I try to spend time at the *House of Enlightenment.* It's not, you know, Disneyland or anything like that. It is peaceful, though.

****

Chelsea and I sit side by side on the steps of the House, sipping tea and enjoying a break from work as we soak up a little sunshine and warmth. The workmen will be here tomorrow to begin hanging the new sign above the door. St. Therese of the Roses will officially be renamed the *House of Enlightenment*, and after that, there will be a huge celebration and official papers transferring ownership from the *ArchDiocese* to the community.

Neither one of us knows what will happen after that. Hopefully good things. With the help of John and Melody to guide us along the way. But the best thing of all, is that, despite everything that's happened, we will be together for as long as the time we are given anyway. I can see her out of the corner of my eye looking at and fiddling with the ring that she let me give her last night. A date hasn't been set yet.

Hopefully, it will be soon.

****

I know Myles can see me fiddling with my ring. I'm too amazed and happy to care, though.

So very much has happened that could have turned everything sidewise. But it didn't. Maybe because we (and our Guardian Angels) wouldn't let it. Or maybe because this was meant to be all along. Best not to examine the hows and whys too closely and just accept things the way they are for now.

Enjoy being happy. And he makes me very happy.....

****

BREAKING NEWS!

In the early hours of this morning, local time, a volcano, long thought to be extinct came to rumbling, roaring, destructive life!

There was little, if any, warning given by the mountain before it blew up.

We are still awaiting details.

We expect the death toll to be in the thousands, and the loss of property and livelihood to cost the country millions of dollars.

There is word that this country's National Guard and military forces are heading there now to assist in the situation.

More information will follow as we receive it.

Now back to your regularly scheduled program...

Tale 18: Long Winter of the Soul

John was off doing John things somewhere. Myles and the rest of the crew, Ramon, Georgi, Karun, Aruna, and the rest are busily rushing around cleaning, putting up new candles, prepping food and a thousand other little things. A work crew from somewhere is hanging a new sign on the House, at the moment carefully concealed. Though it isn't really a secret. There's going to be a big celebration tonight you see. The ArchDiocese had *Finally* made a decision about *St. Therese of the Roses* and the big announcement and reveal was going to happen tonight. Complete with a few fireworks I hear. It seems I'm the only one that isn't ecstatically happy about the whole thing. Which is why I'm sitting up here on the roof alone.

From up here I can see the fifteen square blocks that comprise our "*neighbourhood*". From the hospital to the west, to the business offices at the east end, the nicer houses and apartments to the north and the tenements in the south. And everything in between. Every store, large and small. Every alleyway and dumpster. Every bar and strip joint. Every business man and woman in his or her fancy suit. Every pimp, pusher, prostitute, junkie and homeless person. Every shopper and shopkeeper, janitor, garbage person, labourer and cleaner. Every teacher and student, cop and doctor. And if I concentrate hard enough, the daytime incarnation of D on his rounds.

So, many things that make me proud. So many things that make me hurt.

So, I'm sitting up here in a grey funk, wondering what the point of it all is. Why bother at all?

In the long run, are John and I making a difference?

Is Myles and the rest at the H.O.E.?

For every person that we help, a hundred more make disastrous mistakes or take the wrong fork in the road. The population of homeless people wasn't shrinking. There was an increase in overdoses because it seemed like the only way to escape the hopeless feeling. The hospital was always busy. And on and on and on. A never-ending cycle that seemed to get worse rather than better. *It hurt*. A lot. To think that my function as a Guardian was so pointless. I remembered when

I started, I had been so full of hope. So full of happiness that I had something important to do. I was needed. I felt necessary.

Now I miss the child that I was. The one who didn't think of the wider picture, the wider world. My focus was limited to one thing and only that thing. I had thought of myself as a superhero, writing the wrongs for the people that couldn't do it themselves.

"Huh. Some raise." I think to myself.

"You come early to it, I see," says a voice.

I look around, but there isn't anybody there. Just a slight shimmer in the air. I opt to remain silent. It suited my present mood much better than having a conversation with the Great Unknown would have.

"Most take a lot longer. John has yet to feel it. Possibly never will. And your friend? The one you refer to as D? He had his not too many years ago. Did you know his true name is Desmond by the way? It always amused me that you were so close to the truth of him and never realized it." the voice chuckled a little.

"Desmond's moment of course waited for oh, the better part of two hundred years I believe."

Okay. I'll bite. "What moment is that?" I ask grudgingly.

"The one I generally refer to as the Long Winter of the Soul," it says.

When I didn't respond further (as I'm sure was expected), it continued.

"That moment when you realize how much work still lies ahead of you, and look at what you have done. Then consider the futility of it all. But of course, being what you are, you can't just throw yourself off the ramparts and be done. That way is close to you. Since you've already died once."

For a while there is silence. I get the feeling that he is gazing out at the city, much as I had earlier. I wonder if he sees everything that I do, or more. But I remain close mouthed.

"You know, when Desmond came here the first time, he was technically outside his sphere of influence? His given territory, if you prefer? He should not have been able to do that. But perhaps his need was so grave, and he needed to hear what John told him, that it made no difference. His territory has been rather fluid of late. Maybe because of his methodology, while he performs his task. Maybe because of the man himself. Maybe because of his connection to you. I have no idea. *Strange enough*," another quiet chuckle.

I know what he's trying to do. He wants me to open up and talk. All these little anecdotes are interesting, of course. But they have nothing to do with me, so, stubbornly, I stay silent.

He lets out a great sigh. "A hard case, I see. Very well then. A lecture it shall be rather than a conversation between equals," he pauses, maybe hoping for a response.

Not gettin' it dude. Sorry. Not sorry. I draw my knees to my chin.

"When you look from this lofty height, you see the whole truth of the world you serve. The entire macrocosm of human existence is within these many buildings. The shortcomings. The pain. The confusion. And the joys and hopes and happiness as well. But it seems to you that there is a lack of balance in this. There is a great deal more of one than the other. This wounds you in the deepest places.

There is a reason why you are all given territories, or spheres of influence. The reason is this: you were once a live person, with all the same feelings as everyone down there. You understand this because you know this. It is familiar and safe in its way. Were you to attempt to expand beyond the limits your very human understanding has placed upon you, you would stretch the fabric of yourself to a point of no return. And you would end. Either totally insane and demonic, or failing that, just simply, gone.

Ninety-nine-point nine percent of the people down there can not make any real changes to the world as a whole. But each can change the life of one person that they meet. Perhaps only by smiling. Perhaps by changing their opinion about something. Perhaps by helping in some small way. Perhaps, like Ramon, by keeping people as safe as he can, when he can. But the point is that they affected one person for the better. So the hope is that person will affect another in a similar way. And so on and so forth.

Certainly not everyone will be lucky enough to receive such benevolence, or recognize it for what it is. But a few will. Enough that over time real changes can be seen in this neighbourhood, then perhaps another and another.

That is all that is asked of you as well. Yes, the macrocosm is still there, looming over you. But look closer. Look at the microcosm instead. Think of the people that you have helped in a short time as a Guardian. Georgiana, clean and healthy. Ramon guilt free for his role in things, Junaid free to be himself rather than predestined to a loveless marriage, Rosemary, who was joined by her real daughter at the last and found true peace, Petey and Gina and their little daughter who is even now taking her first steps, your sister Aria, in school taking social work so she can return here to this House and help as she was helped. And a thousand other little things that you haven't even noticed yourself.

This is your true role as Guardian. Not to fix everybody and everything. But to show the people, your people, a way to fix themselves. Some you will succeed with. Some you will not, and for those it is Desmond's role to help them take the next step, whatever that might be for each individual. I could wish for your sake and those like you, that it was more clear cut, that you were able to concentrate more fully on a few rather than so many. But, unfortunately, there is a finite number of persons such as yourself capable, and willing, to become a Guardian. You and the others, are the Elite force between ordinary mortals and what lies beyond and above. But even Elite troops have a limited amount of "ability" at their disposal. So, you must learn to judge wisely and well where you are most needed.

There are people, such as Myles, that are here to help you in that regard. They "free you up" as it were, to work on the more important things, and aim you in the right direction should you get lost along your way. A network. Of people and beings that can think and operate outside the box. Ten small good things are equally as -life-changing- for the microcosm as one huge good thing is for the world. Your limitations are also your strengths. Use them to your advantage. Do not stop thinking about the macrocosm. But do not try to bear the weight of it either. It is unnecessarily dangerous for you.

Remember that you are one of many. Each with, generally, the same weaknesses and strengths as you possess yourself. Narrow your focus. Concentrate on here and what you can do here and now. As best you can. Seek not perfection in this. It does not exist the way you picture it. But try as best you are able. That is more than enough."

And then he is gone. On the upside, I definitely feel a lot better now. It was kind of a relief to know for certain that John and I aren't the only ones out there.

I felt a little foolish too. Had I really been trying to find a way to take responsibility for the whole world? Maybe. Maybe it's another one of those "becoming an adult" things that I wasn't aware of. I really think somebody needs to sit down and make a handbook that explains some of this shit to you. Might avoid a lot of pitfalls along the way if they did.

Whatever.

I guess I'll just keep plugging along. Doing what I can for whoever I can.

OH! And the plus plus?

I can't wait until I see "Desmond" again. I wonder how he'll react when I call him by his real name? Should be good for a laugh or two. *HA HA.*

Some Time Later:

So. Here I am. Basically, back where I started, funnily enough, sitting on top of my building. You know, the one where I lived with my mom. Right next to the alley where I died.

Yeah, that one. So here I sit, the wind blowing by, lifting garbage and paper and pigeon poop off the roof. Watching the people move like ants going about their busy lives. Now I'm older, though, and I hope, wiser. When I first started this journey, I was just a kid. I had no experience, really, with the realities of living. I mean, sure, life with my mother really wasn't all roses and sunshine. But I had food and clothes and stuff that she provided.

Typical kid, I never thought about what she had to do or go through to give us the little bit that we had. Now, though, as I watch, I see. I see the things I never considered before. I feel what never mattered before. I understand, sort of, what it means to be a human being in a world that is determined to beat you down. *Life can be incredibly hard.*

For the prostitute who sells her body because it's the only skill she has to survive. Knowing that it's a dangerous way to live, that she could be the victim of violence. But having no choice. For whatever reason. For the business person who works long, stupid hours at his job, missing time with his family so he can give them all the things that are the best in life. Even though all they really want is him. *Or her.*

For the shopkeeper trying to keep his little business going even though he's out gunned by the big stores. So, he and his family do without sometimes so he can make the payments. For the vendors who sell without building expenses, but still desperately need every dollar they can get. *To live another day.*

For the waiters and waitresses working long, hard hours with aching backs and blistered feet. They smile in spite of the abuse heaped on them by customers (who are probably having a bad day of their own, or just plain mean). For a few measly tips. For the cops and the ambulance drivers, doctors, and nurses that see the worst that people can do to each other and themselves every single day.

For the homeless person, the drug addict, the alcoholic who has surrendered to their inner demons and escapism because they have lost the will to try anymore. But the demons are still there, no matter how much junk, booze, or craziness they use. *You get the picture, I'm sure.*

Yet, for some, there are also moments. Moments of happiness that make the sacrifice worthwhile. Moments that help them turn a corner away from the darkness, back into the sunshine.

There are others who aren't that lucky. Or they are sunk so far into the well of their own misery, they can't feel the sun. Even when it's shining on their faces. So, they try to steal others' sunshine....

As much as I hurt for the "good" ones and ache to help them in every way I can, I still have this simmering anger towards the "bad" ones. Maybe because of Chelsea. I don't know. I started out as a silly human child. I became the embodiment of anger and what I believed was justice. Then John showed me another path and I became a Guardian. *Now?*

Now I would like to avenge all the wrongs ever done to the people I have grown to care about, and the people they care about. And on and on and on. But John says the last thing that anybody needs is an Avenging Angel. That's been tried.

The results were "mixed" he says.

Ramon says he's seen it all. Including vigilante justice. He says all that does is take really good people and bring them down into the horror of the really bad ones. Nobody wins.

So, what am I supposed to do?

What am I supposed to be?

I have all these things I can do. Phenomenal cosmic powers. What good are they?

Revenge, Guard, Avenge. Or chuck it all and be done.

Is a good thing done for a bad reason the same as a bad thing done for a good reason?

I guess it comes down to how it makes me feel inside. If winning makes me feel miserable, what was the point?

I may not be happy with the way some stuff turns out. Maybe neither are the people I'm helping. But I guess we can all hope it works out in the end. We just need to keep trying. Enjoy the sunshine moments when we can get them; a reward for a job well done. And learn from the rest so we don't make the same mistake. Maybe that's all any of us can do. *Powers or not.*

I wonder what Desmond is up to?

Maybe there will be time for a game of checkers or something.

The End

www.ingramcontent.com/pod-product-compliance
Lightning Source LLC
Chambersburg PA
CBHW080605300726
48975CB00011B/2798